Other books by the author:

Starlight

Pit Bull

Overgrown with Love

The Angel of the Garden

A Song for Alice Loom

Eating Mississippi

The Dream of the Red Road

Pulpwood

DREAM
FISHING

SCOTT
ELY

LIVINGSTON PRESS
THE UNIVERSITY OF WEST ALABAMA

Copyright © 2010 Scott Ely
All rights reserved, including electronic text
isbn 13: 978-1-60489-056-3 library binding
isbn 13: 978-1-60489-057-0 trade paper
Library of Congress Control Number 2010929242
Printed on acid-free paper.
Printed in the United States of America,
Publishers Graphics
Hardcover binding by: Heckman Bindery

Typesetting and page layout: Joe Taylor
Cover design and layout: Jennifer Brown
Cover art : The Boatman, 1891 (w/c with pencil on paper)
by Winslow Homer (1836-1910) Brooklyn Museum of Art,
New York, USA/ The Bridgeman Art Library Nationality /
copyright status: American / out of copyright

Proofreading: Susan Ludvigson, Joe Taylor
These stories appeared in the following magazines:
"84 Avenue Foch" Boulevard
"The Poisoned Arrow" Arkansas Review
"Guatemala City" Boulevard
"Lovers of Hurricanes" The Antioch Review
"Dream Fishing" Shenandoah
"Mississippi Rules" Boulevard
"Wasps" Arkansas Review
"The Fishpond" The Antioch Review
"Rocks" Yemassee
This is a work of fiction.
Any resemblance
to persons living or dead is coincidental.

Livingston Press is part of The University of West Alabama,
and thereby has non-profit status.
Donations are tax-deductible:
brothers and sisters, we need 'em.

first edition
6 5 4 3 2 1

TABLE OF CONTENTS

For Susan

DREAM
FISHING

Wasps

CASSIE wanted to play the game naked. It was not that they had not all seen each other naked before. They had gone swimming by moonlight many times off the sandbar where the Mississippi River made a wide gentle loop at the edge of Rembert's father's land. But Cassie at night, the details of her body—breasts, legs, and the patch of hair between her legs—all softened in that gentle light, was not at all how she would look in the glare of a cloudless June afternoon.

"The wasps should have an even chance," Cassie said.

Generations of wasps inhabited a shack on the edge of an enormous soybean field, which lay between the federal levee and the Mississippi. The game they played, invented by Peter and Rembert when they were ten or twelve, was to throw dirt clods at the shack and then run from the enraged wasps. They were proud of their stings. Cassie, who had played the game with them once or twice, preferred not to be stung at all. Peter wondered why now she suddenly wanted to play with no clothes on.

"I never thought of doing that," Rembert said, looking up at a pair of crows flying lazily over the field.

Peter could tell he liked the idea.

"What if she can't keep up?" Peter said. "They'll be all over her."

"She can keep up," Rembert said.

Cassie smiled. It was as if Rembert had just told her she was the

1

most beautiful girl in the world.

It was June and they all had just graduated from high school, Rembert from a boarding school in Ashville and Cassie and Peter from a private day school in Memphis.

Peter was in love with Cassie. He had taken her to the senior prom and to movies in Memphis and once she had let him kiss her. But he knew that meant nothing. She was thinking of Rembert, not him. It was not as if she had ever even gone out on a date with Rembert. When he came home for Christmas or the summer, he went out with other girls. He might go fishing with her, but not to a movie or a dance at the country club.

And when Rembert went off to Harvard in the fall and he went to Tulane because of the scholarship they offered him and Cassie to Ole Miss, nothing would change. Cassie would write to him and he would reply. He doubted if she would write to Rembert, who could not sit still long enough to compose a letter. He wondered if doing battle with the wasps was just a ploy to make Rembert pay attention to her.

"We'll be like Spartan warriors," Rembert said.

As they removed their clothes, it seemed to Peter this was somehow different than swimming off the sandbar in the moonlight. He was anxious, fearing he would get a hard-on, and wondered if Rembert was worried about that too. Cassie stood before them with her small breasts, flat belly, and the patch of blonde hair between her legs.

"You two do look like Greek warriors," Cassie said. "Like on a vase. But I'll bet they were tanned all over."

Rembert struck a stylized pose and they all laughed and Peter knew everything was going to be all right. Rembert did not write letters but Peter was certain he was familiar with the sort of vase she was talking about. Besides excelling at all sports, he had done beautifully in school. He was planning to take a graduate degree in economics so he could advise his father on how to best sell his rice, cotton, and soybeans all over the world.

"Death to Persian wasps!" Rembert shouted.

They took up the chant and started across the field, walking in the furrows between the rows of soybean plants. The soft dark earth felt good beneath Peter's bare feet.

***

It was Cassie who led the attack and not even with a clod of dirt. She had found a flint spear point lying on the top of a pillar of dirt, the way they always found them. He watched the spear point as it left her hand, tumbling in an arc toward a window, and then the thump it made when it hit the floor, and another thump as it hit the wall, which was papered with wasp nests. Every winter they came out on a cold day to see just how many nests were in the shack. Rembert's father wanted to burn the shack down, but Rembert had convinced him to let it stand for a few more years. He and Rembert threw their dirt clods. They all ran.

Out of the corner of his eye he saw Cassie slapping at wasps. Rembert swatted a wasp that was stinging her between her shoulder blades, grabbing her arm as he did it so as not to knock her off her feet. Cassie cried out, whether from another sting or the force of Rembert's hand Peter did not know. So far Peter had not been stung and he was fairly certain Rembert had not either.

They ran to the big poplar in the center of the field. Almost a quarter of a mile from the house, the poplar was a refuge they had learned by experience was beyond the reach of the most enraged wasp. There they lay sprawled on the ground, breathing hard. The wasps had stung Cassie several times, once on her right breast where there was now an ugly red welt. She was not crying, but her nose was running. She covered up one nostril at a time with her thumb and blew the passages clear, just like a man might have done. And then he was sure that all this was play acting, calculated to impress Rembert.

Rembert had been stung once on the leg. He could never recall Rembert crying, not even when as a child he rode his bicycle down one of the gravel access roads to the levee and crashed into a barbed wire fence, from which Peter had had some trouble getting him untangled. He had not made a sound, had not complained except to curse occasionally.

They went to the creek and Rembert showed Cassie how to put mud on their stings.

"It's what the Chickasaws did," Rembert said.

He put mud on her back and Cassie attended herself to the sting on her breast. They did not linger for long at the creek because the mosquitoes were bad. They returned to the field.

"We have to do it again," Cassie said.

"Maybe you've had enough," Rembert said.

Peter realized that by now they had all gotten so used to their nakedness, it seemed natural to them.

"It's what you and Peter do," she said. "You have rules."

The rules were that they threw dirt clods at the shack until both of them received at least one sting.

"You've already got enough stings for both you and Peter," Rembert said.

"We play until Peter gets stung," Cassie said.

"OK, if that's what you want," Rembert said.

All of this was taking on an air of unreality. Peter lay in bed every night and dreamed of holding Cassie in his arms and now here she was naked as in his dreams. He turned from looking at them, still arguing about continuing the game, and gazed across the field at the shack. He again was worried about getting a hard-on. Cassie would be embarrassed and Rembert would laugh and never let him forget it happened.

4

"We'll do it, then," Rembert was saying. "Cassie, don't get so close when you make your throw." He looked off toward the shack. "No, don't you throw. Let Peter do the throwing. He hasn't been stung."

***

Peter approached the shack cautiously, the others twenty yards behind him. He threw the dirt clod and missed the window. It hit the side of the shack, making a cloud of brown dust as it shattered against the weathered boards. The wasps boiled out of the window.

Then Peter was running with Cassie and Rembert in front of him. Peter felt a wasp sting him on the leg. He slapped at it, lost his balance, and fell. One, two, three times he was stung before he could get up and run. And as he ran he felt himself losing the ability to breathe properly. He stumbled and fell again.

This time Rembert saw him fall and came back for him. Peter looked up and there was Rembert standing over him.

"Get up!" Rembert was saying. "Get up! Are you hurt? Get up!"

It was as if they were kayaking at summer camp in Tennessee and he had rolled the boat in the lake and was hanging upside down, looking at the sky and the trees, all distorted through the lens of the water. That was how Rembert's face looked now. He tried to tell Rembert he could not breathe, but all he could manage was a gurgling sound.

Then Rembert was picking him up and he was over Rembert's shoulders, like some deer Rembert had shot, and Rembert was running with him across the field. He could hear the sound of his labored breathing as he ran. Rembert stopped and put him down. Peter lay on his back and looked up at the sky. A thunderhead was building over the river. He heard the horn of a towboat, probably entering the bend around the big sandbar and warning other boats to get out of the way. He heard Cassie saying his name, repeating it over and over like a mantra that would save him.

"He's having an allergic reaction," Rembert said. "I'll go get the jeep."

For a few moments he heard the crunch of Rembert's feet in the soft earth but then that sound was gone. He looked up at Cassie and for the first time noticed that a wasp had stung her on her other breast, just below the nipple.

"It's a stupid game," Cassie said. "A stupid, stupid game."

***

Cassie dressed him while Rembert drove the jeep. They went up on the levee and down off it and onto the highway to Memphis. The wind whipped about through the jeep, making it almost impossible to talk even if he had been able to. He heard a few snatches of conversation as from time to time Rembert asked Cassie how he was doing. They discussed whether it would be better for him to lie down or sit up and finally settled on letting him remain sprawled across the back seat of the jeep, half sitting and half lying down.

They had almost covered the thirty miles to Memphis when it occurred to him for the first time that he might die. He had never told Cassie he loved her, but he expected she knew that.

At the hospital emergency room a shot of epinephrine restored him instantly. But the doctor told him that he could not afford to be stung again. The next time might kill him. He wrote him a prescription for an auto-injector kit he could carry with him in his car or when he was out hunting or fishing.

"Wasps, you say?" the doctor asked.

"Yes, sir," he said. "Big ones."

Then he made up some story about how he had accidentally disturbed a nest.

Cassie and Rembert kept playing the game. He sat in the jeep one afternoon in July and watched them. They had their clothes on but even if they were naked he would have been able to see no details, just the outline of their figures, from where he sat in the shade of the big poplar. Yet at the same time he felt like a voyeur, as if he were lying in the timber at the edge of the sandbar and watching them make love. For she and Rembert had begun to go out on dates. He assumed they were lovers although Rembert never said a word to him about that and he was someone who often talked casually about the girls he slept with.

A thunderstorm was building over the river, the sky above the trees the color of a bruise. The wind tossed the treetops but had not reached the place where he sat in the jeep. Then Rembert and Cassie were running towards him. They had not thrown their dirt clods at the house yet. He saw the rain pursuing them and then catching them so that by the time they reached the jeep they were soaked through. They changed their clothes, Cassie ending up in a set of camouflage Rembert used for turkey hunting. Rembert hardly gave her a second look when they undressed. That made Peter certain they were lovers.

***

He was at Tulane when he got a call from Cassie asking if he would take her to the Tulane-Ole Miss game. She drove down on the Friday night before the game, arriving around midnight. They went to the French Market and had coffee and beignets.

"You haven't been up to see a game with Rembert?" he asked.

"Not worth going," she said. "Any high school in Tunica Country could beat that Harvard team. Rembert says he doesn't go. He goes to New York to watch professional football."

"So you've been up there to see one of those professional

games?"

"No. I haven't been up there a single time and he hasn't come home. He won't do that until Thanksgiving."

He thought how fine it would be if they did not go to the game at all but spent the weekend in the Royal Orleans and had breakfast in bed together in the mornings.

"Rembert wants to get married," she said.

"Now?" he asked.

He felt as if he had stepped in a pool of quicksand while hunting in the swamp. He had hoped Rembert would become interested in some girl at Harvard.

"He's going to quit school and join the army," she said.

"Why would he do that? Married men aren't being drafted."

Peter had been called for a physical. He failed it because of his asthma and his problem with bee stings.

"He says he doesn't want to miss the war," she said. "He wants to serve as an enlisted man, like his great-great grandfather did during the Civil War."

Peter had seen a framed photograph of that grandfather in Rembert's house. It was of a skinny young man, a boy, whose rifle was almost as long as he was. His gaze was fixed and stiff, with eyes like pieces of dark glass.

"But he doesn't have to go if he marries you, if he marries anyone," Peter said.

"He says he has to go," she said. "He's been reading some French writer. André Malraux. Malraux tried to steal bas-reliefs from a Khmer temple in Cambodia. Right after the first world war. Rembert thinks he can do that sort of thing if he goes to Vietnam."

"He could steal art without becoming a soldier. I don't understand. He should stick to selling soybeans and cotton. Why would he want to steal art?"

8

"I don't know. What should I do?"

She was crying now and people at the other tables were watching them. She took some tissue out of her purse and blew her nose.

"Do you love him?" he asked.

Peter wished he had never agreed to meet her. This was a conversation she should be having with her girl friends.

"I think so," she said.

"And he's going to join the army and get himself killed in Vietnam. Are you going to like being a widow?"

Peter was sorry for the words as soon as he spoke them. She had stopped crying. She was sitting there staring at him.

"I mean that could happen," Peter said. "He should be thinking about that. But it won't. You know nothing will happen to him."

He inwardly winced at the emptiness of his words, but the effect upon her was instantaneous. She smiled and brushed some powdered sugar off the sleeve of her dress.

"Yes, he'll be all right," she said. "I know he will."

And then she changed the subject completely, talking instead about how she was going to teach art in elementary school.

She had not gone up to see Rembert, who would have taken her to a professional football game in New York City, a man she said she *thought* she loved. If she saw him, if she slept with him, then she could not deny that he was flesh and blood, helpless as any other man when caught up in the chaos of the war.

He waited for her to raise the subject of whether she should marry Rembert again, but she never did. His belief in Rembert's invulnerability to harm seemed a fact that could not be disputed, like the flow of the Mississippi into the Gulf of Mexico. Then he paid the bill and they left to go get a drink at some bar in the Quarter.

***

The Quarter was filled with students. But they stayed away from the popular bars. They ended up on Royal Street, a little drunk, looking at the furniture in antique shop windows. He imagined her coming to New Orleans with Rembert to buy things after he completed his tour of duty in Vietnam. He expected Rembert would return to school and then go to work for his father. They would have plenty of money to buy antique furniture or anything else they wanted.

She took his hand and drew him from one shop to another. It was easy for him to imagine she was married to him and they were buying furniture for their house.

Then they wandered back into the Quarter and to a bar next to the river. The bar itself had a zinc top. The only customers were three men, all wearing suits with wide lapels. He though they were speaking some sort of Slavic language among themselves. He supposed they were merchant seamen.

He and Cassie sat at a table, and he ordered them a beer.

"I'm not sleepy at all," she said. "Are you?"

"No," he said.

He thought of Rembert lying down to sleep in the mountains of Vietnam or beside a rice paddy. The image of a vine-covered temple appeared in his mind, the façade covered with carvings of strange gods. And there was Rembert directing a group of porters who were carrying off pieces of the gods on their backs. It was a scene straight out of Byron, describing the looting of the Parthenon by Lord Elgin.

"Wait until he comes back," he said.

"What?" she asked.

Surely, he thought, she knew exactly who he was talking about. This was a game she was playing with him.

"Rembert," he said

"Yes, Rembert," she said.

She spoke his name as if it were unfamiliar to her.

"I thought we'd settled that," she said.

"What do you mean?" he asked.

"He won't be killed. I can marry him now."

She was drunk, he thought. They were both a little drunk and it would not be profitable to have a serious discussion about Rembert. But he thought he should say something.

"Cassie, you should think about what you're doing," he said. "This isn't a game."

"Like the wasps?" she said.

"You said it was a stupid game but you've kept on playing it."

"You can't play."

"No, I can't. If I play I might die."

"Oh, you won't die."

He did not think she had drunk so much to become that confused.

"No, you know I could die."

He resolved to steer the conversation somewhere else. But it was difficult for he too was drunk.

"That bed in the shop . . ." he began.

She reached over and put her fingers on his lips. One of the men at the bar turned to look at them, probably sensing there was about to be a lover's quarrel.

"I don't want to go back to the hotel," she said. "I don't want to be alone."

"You can sleep at my apartment," he said.

"Oh, that's sweet of you," she said.

"I'll sleep on the couch."

They got up and left. One of the men at the bar was staring at them. He had a scar on his right cheek, probably the result of a knife fight, yet there was something incongruously cherubic about the man's round face. His thick lips curled into a smile. He said something to one of his companions who turned and looked at them, along with the third man. They all turned back to the bar and laughed. It was as if the man with the scar had overheard Cassie saying that Rembert could not be killed, overheard it and now they all were laughing at the foolishness of the young.

***

His apartment was close to Sophie Newcombe, in one of the old houses not far from St. Charles Avenue. He made them coffee, and they sat together on a sofa. He was using an old trunk he had found in a closet for a coffee table.

"You don't have much furniture," she said.

"Yes," he said. "The room's too big. I can't afford to fill it up."

They drank the coffee, black and thick with chicory, and he felt his head begin to clear.

"Do you want another cup?" he asked.

"No, I won't be able to sleep," she said.

Then he did not know what to say. He wanted to avoid talking about Rembert and suspected she did too. So they talked about school, the classes each of them was taking, and he drank a second cup of coffee. He imagined she was mentally furnishing the room as they talked, for he watched her looking at all that empty space.

She began to yawn and then went off to bed. He was thankful he had a set of clean sheets, sent to him by his mother. He had not bothered to take them out of the plastic they were wrapped in.

He turned off the lights and lay on the couch, hoping a thunderstorm would roll across the city so that she would wake and call out for him like a frightened child. And then she might want him in the bed with her. But it was a warm, still night, filled with the trilling of tree frogs. If the city lights were not there to obscure the view, a person could see a sky filled with stars through the branches of the live oaks. She was sleeping soundly, for he could hear her snoring through the open door.

For what seemed to him a long time he lay awake. When the sound of the traffic from St. Charles had diminished, which meant it was three or four o'clock, he closed his eyes and slept.

***

In the morning it was as if their conversation in the café and the bar had not occurred. They had breakfast and then walked over to Tulane and strolled the campus. She was full of talk about what she and Rembert were going to do after he returned from the war. Her brightness was alarming to him but he said nothing to temper her optimism.

"I don't think I want to go to the game," she said. "I'm going to do some shopping and then drive back to Oxford."

"It's never much of a game," he said.

As they wandered back to his apartment, they both avoided talking of Rembert or home or the war. She talked about furniture for his apartment, and he told her that he had become interested in the history of the troubadours in France.

"They knew something about love," he said.

The instant the words came out of his mouth he regretted speaking them, but she did not take up that theme, talking instead about going to Maison Blanche to shop.

He dropped her off at her hotel where she would go up to the room she had not slept in. She kissed him on the cheek and said that she would write. Through the revolving doors he saw her walking across the lobby for a moment and then she was gone.

***

After the game, he went to a party with some friends. He was determined to enjoy himself, to forget about Cassie, who was surely

13

going to marry Rembert. And he found it disturbing that from time to time he imagined Rembert dead, killed in the war. He imagined the funeral and Cassie dressed in black and he sitting with her in her mother's house after the funeral. And later there would be opportunities to persuade Cassie to fall in love with him.

He met a girl who was from Lafayette and attending Sophie Newcombe. Her parents owned a car dealership in Lafayette.

"I want a martini," Marie said.

He realized he had not had a drink all day. Everyone around him had been doing nothing but that. But it was the sort of party where everyone was drinking Dixie beer or mixing bourbon with Coke.

They went out to buy gin and Triple Sec. Marie wanted to buy it at a liquor store someone had told her about, known as Larry and Kat, but she could not remember exactly where it was. He spent considerable time driving about the grid of streets and asking pedestrians directions while the car was stopped at red lights. No one was able to help them.

They never found the store. They ended up buying the ingredients at an all night drugstore. Marie was disappointed. She wanted to see Larry's black cat, reputed to be always asleep on the counter beside the cash register. Peter was beginning to wonder if the place even existed.

Back at his apartment they made martinis in a shaker he had inherited from an uncle who had been killed during the Normandy invasion. Peter had been using the shaker to store loose change. He would not have bothered to wash it out but Marie complained, saying their drinks would taste of pennies.

He tried not to think of Cassie. But later, after sex with Marie, who was sleeping in the bed, he sat at the kitchen table and drank a cup of coffee. It was already beginning to turn light outside. The birds were singing their morning songs. He liked Marie but he meant to be careful not to end up marrying her or some other girl. He would wait to see if Rembert returned from the war.

It was unnerving to realize that he was going to suspend the normal movement of his life, that he was going to wait to see if his best friend was killed, that there might come a time when he would hope Rembert might be.

When he returned to bed, Marie threw her arms around him. He pleaded a hangover.

"It doesn't matter," Marie said. "It's going to be a wonderful year now that I've found you. You go on back to sleep."

She almost immediately fell asleep again but he did not. He lay on his back, looking up at the water-stained high ceiling with its chipped and cracked plaster as the room filled with morning light. And he suspected that from now on his life was going to be difficult in some unknown and frightening way.

Mississippi Rules

Luther Yelverton had always been on friendly terms with David and his family, so when David asked Luther to teach him how to be a soldier Luther had been inclined to say yes. Luther wondered why David, who was living in France to avoid service in the Israeli army, had suddenly decided to return to Israel and join that army. Israel was not being invaded like during the Six Day War.

"I need training," David said.

"If you go back, they'll throw you in jail for avoiding service," Luther said.

"No, I do not think so."

"Then they'll train you. They're good at it. They have a great army."

"I will be a better soldier if you train me."

"Why do you want to kill Arabs? I thought you liked them."

"I was wrong about them. They wish death for all Jews. They wish to drive all the Jews in Israel into the sea."

"You're going to discover it's not that simple."

"It is. I see it clearly now."

Nothing he could say would dissuade David. Luther considered all the dinners he had eaten cooked by David's mother Elena. So finally he gave up and said yes.

David's wanting to get in shape made sense. But all he needed was to run in the mountains for a month or two and lift some weights. Luther remembered running miles and miles on the Federal levee back in Mississippi just before he went off to join the army during the Vietnam War. It had made basic training much easier.

Luther had come to France long before David and the other artists of Romanian ancestry began to arrive and take up residence on what had once been a fortified farm. The sale of the farm, for a ridiculously small amount of money, had been arranged by the departmental cultural minister. The minister hoped to encourage tourism now that the economy of the region, largely based on textiles, was failing. In every village there were men who spent their days drinking at the local cafes, men who had no hope of finding work. The Romanians were all Jews who had been driven out by Ceausescu. They turned the buildings at the farm into houses and studios.

Luther had come to France after being discharged from the Army as a staff sergeant at the conclusion of his third tour in Vietnam. His company commander had tried to persuade him to stay and had promised him a place in Officer Candidate School. He had received medals for his conduct under fire. He had been wounded twice, first by a bullet through the calf muscle of his right leg and the second time by mortar shrapnel in the chest. The shrapnel left a network of scars across his chest. He never experienced any nightmares or suffered in any way from the experience. From time to time the shrapnel scars itched. That was his only complaint.

Now in his middle age he looked back on the war with a sort of pleasant nostalgia. If he had joined at some other time, he probably would have been sent to language school because of his degree in French. But instead he became an infantryman. He had fought in the mountains where there were no civilians or villages, where there was nothing to confuse the issue. The Americans were on the ridge tops; the North Vietnamese Army was in the valleys and gorges.

Once he even had the opportunity to use his French. He had a brief conversation with a North Vietnamese colonel before the man died of his wounds. Luther was supposed to be extracting information from him. Luther's captain, who spoke no French, stood and watched as the colonel talked about a girl he had loved in Paris when he was there as a student. Luther reported to the captain that what the man said made no sense at all.

Instead of going back to his father's farm in the Mississippi Delta and helping to grow cotton, soybeans, and rice, he had taken his combat pay from those three tours and gone to Paris. He intended to study at the Sorbonne, but he never got around to it. He stayed in Paris, living in cheap places. He went to museums and read books. He pursued girls and watched his money slowly dwindle.

His father wrote him a few letters and Luther sent him one or two sentence replies written on postcards with pictures of Notre Dame or Place Vendôme on them. He and his father had fallen out over his joining the army. They had earlier clashed over his degree in French. His father's dream had been for Luther to take over the running of the farm. He had wanted him to go to the state agricultural college instead of Ole Miss. But Luther hated farming. His father had told him that he could get him into the National Guard. When he refused, his father had called him a fool.

Luther did not completely understand why he had joined the army. He recalled he had imagined himself on leave in Saigon speaking French to waiters at the cafes on the broad boulevards. But that had never happened. He had been in a Vietnamese town on only one occasion. It was Pleiku during the Tet Offensive of 1968. His visit to a brothel ended in a firefight with the local Viet Cong.

His mother had died when Luther was a child. He had no

brothers or sisters. Now his father had remarried. When his father died, childless from the second marriage, Luther imagined he and the wife would fight over the farm if there was anything left to fight over. He suspected his father was deeply in debt.

His first year in France he made friends with Laurent, a student at the Sorbonne. Laurent was studying American literature and was interested in William Faulkner. He asked Luther to explain passages from *The Sound and the Fury* but Luther was never able to give Laurent any help with the meaning of those convoluted sentences. Laurent would soon graduate and was planning to go to a small village not far from Carcassonne and build an indoor court where he could teach tennis. Laurent had been a top ranked junior player but an injury to his foot when he was fourteen had ended his career. He could run but he could not jump. Luther had played on the tennis team at Ole Miss. He and Laurent had met at the courts in the Luxembourg Gardens.

It had been almost thirty years since he and Laurent had gone into business together. Laurent's father had friends in the government who made it easy for Luther to obtain a long-term visa. In a tiny village in the foothills of the Pyrenees, just off the highway to Carcassonne, they built an indoor court and two squash courts and an outdoor court. They planned to teach tennis to the sons and daughters of the middle class people of a nearby town and the surrounding villages.

***

It was July. Luther and Laurent's regular tennis students had gone off on summer vacations. Their students were now mostly foreigners, Dutch and German, who came to the region to hike and bicycle in the Pyrenees. To keep up the payments on the tennis complex Luther and Laurent had to give many lessons. They had borrowed money against their equity several times to resurface the

19

courts and once to repair the roof, which had been blown off by a violent mistral. It seemed to Luther that they were never going to get clear of the bank. Laurent had married for a third time. He and his young wife had two small children. Luther at the moment did not have a girl friend. Germaine had left in June to take a job in Paris. She had wanted him to come with her but he had refused. He liked imagining what the next woman he lived with might be like. So at the first opportunity he let his girlfriends go.

Luther ended the day by giving a lesson at a tourist camp where the campers were mostly Dutch. The owner of the camp raised chickens on the court during the rest of the year. It was a hard court and now by the middle of July the surface was mostly free from the white splotches left by the chickens.

After his lesson he drove over a ridge on the narrow winding mountain roads to the fortified farm. It was built on the banks of a tributary of the Aude. There were green fields of corn and fields of sunflowers whose heads were turned towards Spain. Looking at the fields, spread out across what in Mississippi would be called a creek bottom, Luther was always reminded of home.

David's parents, both engineers, had left Israel when David had decided not to go into the army. Michael and Elena had fled Romania during the reign of Ceausescu, before David was born, and had become Israeli citizens. David still lived with his parents, who were both retired. Elena coddled her thirty year old son. David had warned Luther to say nothing about the training to his parents.

**

Elena came out of the house and waved to him when he drove up. The yard was filled with David's work. He worked mostly in wood, but lately had been doing some things in bronze. Sometimes Luther thought the objects David made of peeled fir logs looked too much like playground equipment.

20

He had met David when he had given him tennis lessons at a court in a nearby village. David was athletic but too eager to hit the ball hard. He seemed almost pleased when some of the balls Luther fed him sailed over the fence and into the creek that ran behind it. Luther imagined the balls carried by the creek down from the mountains and past the battlements of Carcassonne and into the Rhône and finally into the blue waters of the *Golfe du Lion*.

David came out of the house with a mountain bike over his shoulder. Elena walked over to the car as they were putting David's bike up on it.

"Be careful," she said. "A German tourist was killed on the road last week."

"We're going to ride in the forest," Luther said.

"Good," she said. "Good."

She gave David a kiss on the cheek. As she kissed him, an image of Luther's own mother, who had died when he was eight years old, suddenly filled Luther's mind, her appearance as startling to him as a parachute flare opening overhead and illuminating the bush with its hard white light. She, dressed in white, was hitting tennis balls with him at Highlands late on a summer afternoon in the North Carolina mountains. She was fair and her skin tanned beautifully, like one of those models in ads for suntan lotion. That night, after she kissed him as she tucked him into bed, the smell of her hand cream lingered in his mind into the edge of sleep. Now as he drove down the dirt track to the paved road, he smelled it again, as if her hands were actually pulling the blanket up over him as she sat beside him. He had wanted her to stay, just as Proust had wanted his mother to stay. But then she was gone and he was left with the smell, which he thought was lilac. In the morning she had died of a heart attack on the tennis court while he slept.

They drove up into the fir forest, the *Forêt de Puivert*, and turned off the paved road onto a dirt track loggers used to bring timber out of the forest. The road stopped where a bulldozer had pushed up a heap of dirt. They got out of the car and Luther took from the trunk the .22 caliber rife he had borrowed from a neighbor. David had never shot a gun of any kind.

He explained to David how the semi-automatic rifle worked and how to mount it on his shoulder. Then he set up beer cans as targets on the berm. David learned quickly and soon he had shot the beer cans to pieces. He was eager to shoot a military weapon, but Luther saw little chance of getting their hands on an assault rifle.

"Learning to hunt is more important," Luther said. "How not to walk into an ambush."

That had helped to keep him alive in Vietnam. Only one or two of the other boys in his platoon had been hunters. Most never became comfortable on the rain forest-covered mountains.

"How are you going to tell your mother you're going back to Israel?" Luther asked.

"I am not," David said. "She will think that I have gone to Japan for an exhibition."

"What if you don't like what you become."

"I will become a soldier. That is honorable. I realized I had to decide what side I was on. It was necessary to choose."

***

In the weeks that followed, Luther rode a bicycle as he accompanied David on runs over the mountain roads. David told his mother he was training for tennis. Luther taught David how to walk quietly in the forest. They practiced stalking deer, the stags that lived in the mountains. They were regularly hunted so the bucks were wary. The day they walked up on a big stag together Luther knew they were making progress. The breeze shifted and the stag scented them. It went crashing away through the tangle of bushes and nettles that was as dense in places as any swamp in Mississippi.

They also practiced on the dry side of the mountains where there were no firs. Here the land was covered with a blanket of aromatic herbs and evergreen shrubs. It had a desert feel to it. They set up ambushes for hikers who passed on trails before them and never knew the two of them were there, crouched in the shrubs. It was hot. There were biting flies. David complained, but Luther told him he had to learn to endure. He had to learn to be patient.

***

Luther got a call from Germaine, who told him she was pregnant. She was going to have the child.

"I have had three abortions," she said. "Twice with you. I am sick of doing that."

Germaine was thirty-eight. He could understand why she wanted a child. He told her he would go to the *Mairie* and sign the papers to legally acknowledge the child as his.

He invited her to come down for her vacation. She was delighted and said she would come for the whole month of August. He was pleased she had not talked about marriage.

***

He picked up Germaine at a rural train station halfway between Toulouse and Carcassonne. A company of young paratroopers wearing their red berets was waiting to board the train. Their regiment was stationed in Carcassonne. They were wheeling each other up and down the station platform in the baggage-handling carts, yelling and laughing like children on a holiday from school.

Germaine, who was tall and dark, was a social worker. He could recall her and David having discussions over the ill treatment of Arabs in France. Then they were in agreement and often enjoyed baiting those on the right who wanted to send all the Arabs back to the homes of their ancestors. Such sentiment was popular in the region.

As they drove through the countryside he told her of David's plan.

"And you are helping him," she said.

"He asked me," he said. "I thought of all those dinners Elena's cooked for me."

"Elena will be very angry with you."

"She won't find out."

"Well, I think it is quite a bad idea."

She began to talk of her plans for the child. He wondered if in the end she was going to press him to marry her. But he believed he knew how to avoid marriage.

At his house they had coffee on the balcony. The weather had turned a little cooler, and they were comfortable as long as they sat in the shade. It seemed to him it was as if she had never left. He wondered if she was thinking the same thing. She talked about her job in Paris, a promotion that came with more money. She felt she was doing important work.

They went out and bought a fish for dinner. She bought flowers for the planter on the balcony. The ones that had been there when she left had died from his neglect. They cooked dinner together and ate late. The mountains over towards Spain loomed dark against the sky at the other side of the narrow valley.

Around ten o'clock a rock band began to play in the village square. Over the rooftops they could see the lights from the graveled court by the small lake where every night old men played *boule*. In the square was the usual monument to the dead of World War I. It appeared to him that the war had taken the whole village.

He thought of Laurent, who was in his house not far away, sleeping with his wife and children. Luther wondered what that would feel like, to go to sleep with his child sleeping in the house.

"You should stop training David," she said. "What if he goes to Israel and is killed?"

"He's a man, not a boy," Luther said. "He can make his own choices."

Luther thought of those boys, the ones during his second and third tours when he had been in command. He had made choices that had resulted in their deaths. But he had used those boys wisely, had not taken reckless chances with their lives. He had been with them taking the same risks. He was with some of them when they died, a few stoically but others calling out for their mothers. He said none of this to her because he knew she would not understand.

"Just think of how difficult it will be to explain his death to Elena," she said.

"Israel is not at war," he said. "There'll be little chance of anything happening to him."

"It is not as simple as you wish it to be."

"I know."

"If you know then it is all right."

They sat there in the darkness and he drank wine, while she drank bottled water. She had given up wine because of the child. They talked the way people who have been intimate with each other for a long time talk, casually and relaxed, sometimes already knowing what the other's response will be. It was pleasant for him to talk like that with her. They talked until the band stopped playing and the lights at the *boule* court went out.

They went to bed and made love under the mosquito netting. He lay there awake beside her for a long time while she slept, and thought about her leaving at the end of August. After she left it would not be long before another woman would be living in the house with him. He tried to imagine who she would be and what she would be like. Finally he drifted off to sleep.

He dreamed of his mother. They were on that tennis court in the mountains. He had a grocery cart full of balls and he, a young man, was feeding them to her. She moved from side to side. She never seem to tire, and the supply of balls in the cart was inexhaustible. His arm became tired and the grip on his racket slick with sweat. It was as if he were playing a match. She had a smile on her face. He realized she was not becoming fatigued because she was flying, her feet suspended a few inches above the surface of the court. Then she soared over the trees and disappeared. He stood there gasping for breath and calling out for her.

***

Luther bought two BB guns in Carcassonne. They were designed to mimic a lever action Winchester and had a picture of a cowboy on a horse cut into the wooden stocks. His first gun had been a BB gun like one of these. He and his friends had played at war, hunting each other in the woods between the Federal levee and the Mississippi River. It had been just luck that no one had lost an eye during those games. A hit meant you were dead, and shooting at someone above the waist was against the rules. Two of those boys had not survived the war.

At a war surplus store he bought two sets of camouflage fatigues and camouflage paint. The man behind the counter made a joke about him joining the Foreign Legion at his age. He was older than Luther and was dressed in a sleeveless t-shirt to show off his big arms and chest. His muscles were just beginning to lose their definition and elasticity. The man had worked hard at caring for his body.

"I was too old at twenty," the man said. "At Dien Bien Phu I discovered I was too old."

Luther had lunch at a Vietnamese restaurant across the street from the headquarters of the airborne regiment. He sat at a table under the shade of a plane tree and watched the soldiers go in and out. There was an armed guard at the gate. The soldiers, dressed in shorts and running shoes, went off to run together in twos and threes. He could imagine them spending hours lifting weights. They were adding layers of muscle to their chests and strengthening their legs so that when the time came their bodies would respond in the ways necessary to keep them alive.

Two sergeants came in to have lunch. They chatted familiarly with the owner, a woman about Luther's age, from Saigon. It turned out the younger one was engaged to her niece. As they waited for their food, they talked about a training exercise they were going to hold the next week in the *Forêt de Puivert*. A platoon under the command of the older sergeant was going to hunt a squad led by the younger sergeant. The squad had to work their way from a valley to the top of a mountain where they would be extracted by helicopter at night. The platoon would be dispersed over the mountain to block their approach. The exercise, which would take place over three days, was scheduled to start the following Wednesday. The sergeants made a bet over the outcome.

***

Luther met with David the next day and they drove to the forest. It was hot. The temperature in Carcassonne was close to a hundred but it was cooler in the mountains. David began to practice with the BB gun. They called the training "quick kill" in the army. Soldiers were trained to shoot at metal disks tossed in the air a few feet away. They were taught not to use the sights but to point the gun. It was like shooting quail. Luther had done plenty of that and already knew what his instructors were trying to teach him. Now Luther used beer cans instead of metal disks. David caught on fast.

They put on the uniforms and painted their faces. Luther told David to follow a stream up the mountain and set up an ambush. It would be Luther's job to find him and hit him with a BB before he could do the same to Luther. Mississippi rules.

"Be patient," Luther said. "Think of nothing but the forest."

David walked off into the trees and began to work his way up the stream, which at this time of the year was completely dry. In twenty minutes Luther would follow.

As Luther sat on the hood of the car and waited for the time to pass, he thought of how in Vietnam he would sit at twilight, waiting for it to get dark, and watch the ducks sail overhead as they went to roost in the paddy fields beside the river. They were big ducks, similar to mallards, and often he wished he had a shotgun in his hands. Then it would grow too dark to see them, but he could still hear the whistle of their wings. Soon after that he would send the point man out and they would start walking.

David's time had run out. Luther walked into the woods. After he had gone a few hundred meters, he turned at a right angle to the stream bed and walked up and over the ridge. Now, hidden by the ridge line, he walked parallel to the stream. It was hard going and at times he had to crawl. There were briars and some sort of low shrubs covered with thorns. It always made him uncomfortable that he did not know the names of the plants, and the bird songs were a mystery to him, not like in Mississippi where he knew the name of every tree and the song of every bird.

He walked until he was sure he had gone farther than David was likely to have walked. He turned back toward the stream bed. When he was halfway down the crest of the ridge, he began to crawl. It was slow, but a man walking made too good a target. From time to time he stopped and listened. But the only sounds he heard were the tops of the firs being stirred by a gentle breeze and the songs of the birds.

Just as he worked his way down to the dry creek bed and was slipping around the side of a large, moss and lichen-covered boulder, he came upon a snake that had killed and eaten a small animal. The snake, whose markings were dark and muted, lay flaccid in a open space surrounded by the thorny shrubs. The animal, probably a rat, made a bulge midway down its body. When he crawled past, the snake's only acknowledgement of his presence was to slightly turn its head in his direction.

There was much less vegetation in the creek bed, and the boulders provided plenty of cover so he no longer had to crawl. He supposed David was looking downstream, guarding the obvious approach.

During one of the periods when he stopped and lay still and listened, he thought he heard a sound that did not belong in the forest. Then it disappeared before he could really identify it, leaving only the songs of the birds. A gang of ravens swooped over the treetops. One lighted in the top of a fir for a few moments before it flew off to join the rest, their calls fading into the distance as they flew over a ridge.

He continued down the creek bed, stopping even more often to listen. Then he heard it again, a sort of watery sound. He wondered if he thought it was watery just because he was in the creek bed. It stopped. He crawled up out of the creek bed onto the left hand side of the creek. He had gone only a few meters when he heard it again on the other side of a boulder. Now he realized it was no animal, but David, who had gone to sleep on his ambush position and was snoring. He had awakened boys in the rain forest before who had gone to sleep when they were supposed to be watching a trail. He usually made them take amphetamines supplied by the army. He never used them because the pills gave him hallucinations. One night, high on the speed as he lay in an ambush position on the flank of a mountain, he had watched his mother walk past on the trail. He had seen her clearly, her body illuminated by a greenish light like the glow of a firefly's tail. Then she was gone and it was perfectly dark again on the mountain.

He crawled around the side of a boulder. David, who had leaned his BB gun up against a big fir, was sitting with his back against the tree. Luther had told him that at all times he should be in physical contact with his weapon. Luther stood up and took aim at David's leg. He hoped at this range the BB might even penetrate the skin, for the fatigues were made of light material. It all depended on the angle, and he tried to align the gun so the BB would hit the fleshy part of the calf at a right angle. He pulled the trigger.

David gave a yelp and grabbed his leg.

"You're dead," Luther said.

"You shot me," David said.

He was pulling up the leg of the fatigues. Luther knelt beside him. There was an indentation in his calf and a little blood. The BB had fallen out of the wound.

"You went to sleep," Luther said.

"I thought you were lost," David said.

"Why'd you think that?"

"I do not know."

"You must concentrate. You must stay alert. Concentrate like you do on your sculpture."

"I think it is time to go home."

"You don't want to do this."

"No, it is necessary for me to learn. You are a good teacher. I will never go to sleep again."

Luther saw again how crazy all this was. He had no business training David to be a soldier. But maybe David would get it out of his system. Besides, it was too late now to tell David he was quitting.

"Then follow me back to the car," Luther said. "You move the way I move. Make no noise."

David did a good job and paid attention to where he was putting his feet. Then they were back at the car where they cleaned off their face paint.

"I now understand," David said.

He had his pants leg rolled up and was examining the wound made by the BB.

"I was thinking of making something out of that tree I went to sleep against," David said. "I was dreaming the shape of it. Then I fell asleep. Now that I know it can happen it will not happen again."

"Good," Luther said.

As he drove David home, Luther thought of his mother appearing on the trail so long ago. He had waited for the trip flares to go off but nothing had happened. He was pleased with her incorporality, pleased she was no more substantial than colored gas in a glass tube.

***

Luther and Germaine had dinner on the balcony that night. Hawk moths swooped about the flowers. He told her about his dream of his mother and how he had seen her in Vietnam.

"You never told me about her," she said.

"Suddenly she is on my mind," he said.

"Why?"

"I hadn't thought about my mother's death for a long time."

He explained to her how his mother had died.

"It was a waking dream. She was putting me to bed, the night before she died. It happened when I went to pick up David. I was starting his training. It was so real. I smelled the scent of her hand lotion again."

"What is her connection for you with the war?"

"I don't know."

They were both silent for a time. Then they began to talk of visiting one of the caves whose walls were covered with paintings

31

of bison and deer. It was going to be a hot day. The interior of the cave was always cool.

***

Luther told David they were going to hunt the paratroopers on the mountain. Their object would be to work themselves into a good ambush position just as the squad was being extracted. David would tell his parents he was visiting friends in Toulouse.

Luther told Germaine of his plan.

"It is crazy what you are doing," she said.

"They'll never know we're there," he said.

"That is not what I mean. Is this something you need to do? Are you remembering the war in this way?"

"No, I'm not thinking about the war at all."

"Then why are you doing it?"

"So David can become a soldier."

"I do not think that is the reason. It is something else."

He thought about her speculation as to his motives as he walked on the mountain with David. He and David carried packs filled with dehydrated fruit and a water filter. They would use the filter to take water out of a tributary of the Aude that ran through a narrow gorge they would have to cross. They would build no fires and show no lights as they attempted to slip through the platoon and then ambush the squad as the helicopter came in to retrieve them. The mountains were not all fir trees. There were meadows scattered across them where sheep grazed in the summer. That was the nature of the game. Figuring out which meadow a helicopter would use and when it would make the extraction. The older sergeant did not have enough men to watch all possible landing zones.

They spent the first day going up the mountain and slept that night under the firs. It was a warm beautiful night and since they had not made any contact with either the platoon or the squad,

Luther did not bother setting up four hour watches. They both slept well.

The next day they went down into the gorge and located a squad from the platoon. The boys were filling their canteens from a pool in the stream. They were easy to spot because they were making noise. Luther led David several hundred meters upstream. They crossed the stream and worked their way ahead of the squad.

Luther had studied topographical maps of the forest. It was obvious what general path the squad would have to take to slip past the platoon. There was only one good way up onto the flank of the mountain where the meadows were. The young sergeant knew it and so did the sergeant commanding the platoon. The older sergeant would have set up ambushes on every trail.

The second night they slept at the base of three huge rocks that from the highway looked like a chair. This night Luther set four hour watches. From where they lay down to sleep among the firs they could not see the lights of the cars on the highway. A trail ran up behind the rocks and over a ridge. Somewhere on it there was surely an ambush.

Luther was watching the trail and listening to David breathe in a heavy, slow rhythm. Luther did not feel sleepy at all. He found himself wishing he would see his mother walking past him, her body illuminated by that green light. He felt uneasy, even afraid, but he was not sure what he had to fear. This was only an exercise, a game. When he had done it for real, he recalled, he had been afraid, and he had calmed his fear with the ancient trick of telling himself the worst that could happen was that he could be killed.

He heard something on the trail. A man appeared. He moved slowly. Then he stopped and signaled with his hand. Another man appeared. Slowly the squad went past them. When they turned off the trail and struck out through the undergrowth, where it was impossible to move without making noise, he was certain it was the squad led by the young sergeant. Not walking the trail was a maneuver designed to avoid possible ambushes.

Luther closed his eyes and brought up a picture of the mountain in his mind. They were going to walk a narrow ridgeline that would take them to a spot below one of the meadows. There they would rest and the next night climb up the cliff face. They would locate the squad that lay waiting for them and pretend to kill them, just as he had pretended to kill his childhood friends in Mississippi. Luther wondered if David could make the climb with him. This would not be a good time to find out David was afraid of heights.

He lay down to sleep. Now that he knew exactly what they were going to do it made sense to be rested for what lay ahead.

***

The vegetation was thick along the ridgeline. They had to crawl as often as walk, and he admired the squad for doing it at night. They followed a trail marked by broken branches. Once he found a piece of a uniform on a thorn bush. It took them all day to come close to the base of the cliff. They stopped and waited for dark. He was going to give the squad plenty of time to make their way up the cliff. It was a climb of fifty meters but one he thought they could make without the use of ropes.

They had only a little water left. He told David to save it for just before they began their climb.

"Am I doing well?" David asked.

"You are becoming a good soldier," he said.

David had done well. He had not complained, and he had moved through the forest quietly.

They lay in the shade until it grew dark. He imagined if a squad lay in wait at the meadow, they would not be guarding this approach. He guessed that the sergeant would move his men up the cliff until they were close to the top and then send one man to find the location of the ambush. That would take a long time. It would be close to morning before they would be ready to call in the helicopter.

At dark, after they drank the rest of their water, he led David to the foot of the cliff and they started up. It turned out to be an easy climb. David was a good climber who moved quietly and made no mistakes. They stopped halfway and waited. His plan was to listen for movement from above. He and David did no talking but communicated by signs. He knew that the men above them were doing the same.

A little after three o'clock in the morning they heard a small stone someone had dislodged come bouncing down the cliff face. Then for a long time there was silence. Finally Luther heard the sound of men climbing. They were careful and the sounds of their feet on the boulders were faint, but he heard them distinctly.

They followed the squad, who were not likely to be listening for someone climbing below them. Then they were at the top. Through a stand of firs planted in orderly rows was a patch of lighter darkness which marked the meadow.

David tapped him on the shoulder and pointed out toward the valley. He cupped his hand over his ear. Then Luther heard the sound of the helicopter. They were both looking through the trees, trying to spot the helicopter, when automatic weapon fire suddenly broke out on the far side of the meadow where one group was shooting blank cartridges at the other. He led David to the edge of the meadow. The helicopter was making its approach, coming in with no lights. A group of men darted out of the trees toward it and scrambled aboard. The young sergeant had won his bet. They stood at the edge of the meadow and watched the chopper lift off.

"We could've destroyed it as it lifted off," he said. "They had no idea we were here."

"I performed well?" David asked.

"You were perfect."

"It was difficult."

"Yes, but you did all I asked of you."

They walked out across the meadow, careless now of exposing themselves to enemy fire. On the far side they found the dirt track where a farmer brought his equipment in to cut and bale hay. The track connected with a gravel road that led down the mountain.

On the way they caught up with the squad who had been ambushed. "You are playing at being a soldiers?" a young soldier asked.

"I will soon be a soldier," David said.

Luther explained how he had used the soldiers' war games to help with David's training. David told them about his plans to join the Israeli army. Some of the soldiers offered advice on how to prepare himself and shared their water with them.

The soldiers were not happy with their defeat. It meant they had to walk back to their trucks. The winners were probably by now almost back at Carcassonne.

Luther felt elated by their success yet at the same time it was disturbing to remember lying beside the trail and wishing he could catch a glimpse of his mother. If that had not happened, the three days would have been perfect. He thought that if he ever went back to America he would travel to Highlands to see if the tennis court was still there. He was not sure what he expected to feel if he returned and stood on it one June morning.

***

David had an accident in his studio and was taken to the hospital in Carcassonne. He had dropped molten bronze on his foot. Luther and Germaine went to visit him. The doctors had been able to save his foot.

"The doctors say I will be like Laurent," David said.

"The Israeli army will have to do without you," Germaine said.

"I think it was foolish for me to become a soldier," David said.

"And hate Arabs," Germaine said.

"You cannot love the people you kill," David said.

It appeared to Luther that David was truly relieved the accident had solved his ethical problem for him.

"I will train you for tennis," Luther said. "You can do that."

"Yes, Laurent will be my model," David said.

Elena came in. They talked for a while and then said goodbye. They left the hospital and walked along the sidewalk.

"Do you think he will change his mind and go to Israel?" she asked. "He could drive a truck or a tank."

"It will be a long time before the foot heals," he said. "He will have time to think."

They reached his car. Two small boys were playing on the sidewalk. They were having a sword fight, using the plastic swords and shields that were sold everywhere in the old city behind those fairy tale battlements.

Luther thought about teaching his child to play tennis. Perhaps that was what he would do if he ever returned to Highlands, play tennis on the court with his child. That night he wanted to talk with Germaine again about his vision of his mother. She thought it was connected with the war in some way. But they had the rest of August to talk about that. He was in no hurry. Maybe he would not talk about it at all.

At the end of the month she would leave. He would not think at all about her. He would not try to imagine the shape of her breasts or the curve of her hips. He would lie with some new woman beneath the mosquito netting while his child grew inside Germaine. He would dream no dreams of the war or of his mother.

His life would be the same as it had always been. He wanted it to be that way.

The Fishpond

SAM Ferguson met the new maid for the first time when he came in from setting traps for the otters that were eating his wife Monica's Japanese carp. He had yet to catch an otter in one of the humane traps. He had not told her that today the otters had taken a carp out of a pond over which he had stretched netting. They had simply tunneled under it. She had paid five hundred dollars for that particular fish. And besides, she had grown attached to them. She gave them names from *The Tale of Gengi* and other pieces of Japanese literature.

"Good morning, Mr. Ferguson," she said. "I'm Mrs. Pack."

Her familiarity, the way she spoke his name and announced hers, made it seem as if this woman he had never set eyes on before had been working for them for years. Skinny and missing a couple of teeth, she looked to be well into her sixties. She had obviously had a hard life. She could be much younger, maybe in her early fifties like him and Monica. Now she was staring at him in a peculiar way.

He said good morning to her and she smiled, revealing more bad teeth.

"You catch any otters?" she asked. "Any coons?"

He imagined her interview with his wife. He wondered what topics they had covered besides the otters. Monica liked to talk. What had Monica told her about him that the woman found so amusing?

"Not a one," he said.

She was looking him in that way again, a slight smile on her lips.

"I've got a cousin in Memphis who could catch those otters," she said. "He works on race cars."

She mentioned the name of a race car driver that meant nothing to him. Was there a connection he was supposed to make between the man's being a fine mechanic and his ability to catch otters?

Monica and this woman would get along splendidly. Most people would have just offered the services of the cousin. If he lingered in the kitchen, he would find out what the cousin preferred for Sunday dinner.

"We just may have to give him a call," he said.

"Mrs. Pack," he heard Monica call.

Mrs. Pack smiled and slid out of the room, her running shoes soundless on the tile floor. "Slid" was the right word, he thought. She looked too languid to be any good at cleaning.

He went into his office and closed the door behind him. He turned on his computer and began to research the habits of otters. She had not been in to clean it yet. The wastebasket was full; the desk was covered with dust. There was always dust in the house these days because of the drought. It had not rained all summer, the river dried up to a few pools. No wonder the otters had come up to the fishponds to eat the carp. No doubt they had young otters to feed.

Now he wished that when he and Monica had sold their business (a company that provided elaborate tents for functions like weddings and golf tournaments), he had not allowed her to persuade him to buy the property just below Memphis. It had originally been built as a therapeutic hospital for children with polio. The original owners had named it Cypress Springs. Springs fed the fishponds, but the water did not emerge from among a stand of cypresses. He wondered why they had not at least planted some. But perhaps the original cypresses had died, victims of some previous drought. There was the huge rambling house, a barn, the fishponds, and a few crumbling outbuildings of uncertain purpose. They lived in a wing of the house they had renovated. But the best thing about the property was a screened-in swimming pool with frescos made of colored tile on the bottom and sides depicting scenes that one would expect to see on a Grecian vase: satyrs in pursuit of nymphs, warriors afoot and on horseback, a sacrificial procession toward a temple on a hill. Did the children swim among them? Perhaps the tiles were added by a later owner. The pool was his favorite place. He swam laps in it every day.

But lately he had found that he was uncomfortable living on the property. Monica had led him to believe she was interested in raising horses. How had those horses turned into fish? And he had wanted to paint. That was the primary reason he had retired early. Neither of them had wanted children, and one of the rewards for that decision had been early retirement. Now they had lived on the property for two years. He had plans for turning some of the empty space in the unused wing, once a dormitory for the children, into a studio. Instead he had spend his time supervising workmen during the renovation, and now his job seemed to be to protect Monica's fish from the otters. He had done no painting.

There was a knock on the door. It was Mrs. Pack. As she emptied the trash basket, he did not turn his head to look at her. But he was thinking about her cousin. Perhaps he was what they needed to rid themselves of the otters.

***

Monica cried when he told her about the loss of the carp she had named Lady Fujitsubo. They had both thought the net would do the job. It crossed his mind that a joke could be made about the difficulty an otter might have in eating a fish with a name that long. But Monica was in no state for jokes. He might mention that to Mrs. Pack's cousin. They would both laugh.

"We'll put them in the pool?" Monica said.

"They'll need fresh water," he said.

"Well, drain it and fill it again," she said. "They won't be able to get into that."

Luckily, because of the springs, there was no problem with water. Even now, at the height of the drought, the water gushed out of them. As he contemplated that he realized there would have been no chance of cypresses dying in some previous drought. Someone had chosen the name simply because it was evocative. Of funerals? No, they were not thinking of funerals. This was a place where children came to overcome their brush with a deadly disease, to rebuild their withered limbs. It was a place of hope.

He thought about the difficulties of managing the pool for the carp. So he told her about Mrs. Pack's cousin. But Monica was not interested in harming the otters. She said that she just could not do that.

"Mrs. Pack is from Mississippi," she said.

She named a small town close to the state university where he had gone to school. He was not surprised at Mrs. Pack's journey to Memphis. That's what people like Mrs. Pack did. They finished high school (or maybe they did not finish high school) and then they moved to Memphis to find work. But there was not much work there either so they ended up on welfare or took menial jobs.

"So when could you do it?" she asked.

"What?" he asked.

She reminded him that they were talking about putting carp into the swimming pool.

"Tomorrow," he said.

42

It was two weeks before he got around to draining the pool and refilling it. He had buried some wire fencing around the perimeter of the fishpond, and so far the otters had been stymied. But Monica had made it clear the fish were going into the swimming pool. She had ordered a new carp over two feet long. He had not asked what it cost, but he knew it must have been several thousand dollars. It was a white fish with a single red spot on its head. She had printed out a photograph of it from her computer and placed it on the refrigerator. She was still thinking about a name for the fish and from time to time tried out various ones on him. But he was no help to her. He liked all of them. He was not interested in names. Instead he was concerned about the wire he had buried. Had he done a good job? He was not willing to trust the fishpond's defenses against the otters when the life of such an expensive fish was at stake.

Mrs. Pack, who had come and gone twice, turned out to be the best maid they had ever employed. It was hard to find a speck of dust in the house. She had not engaged him in conversation again. She seemed to him to flow, not walk, silently about the house. After she finished her work, she and Monica had long conversations over coffee.

As he watched the pool finally fill to the top, he decided that he would take a swim in it. There was no reason he could not continue his swims. He supposed that the fish would get used to his presence. He stripped off his clothes. He always swam naked. And always, down at the bottom of the pool, where the nymphs were pursued by satyrs, he would have a beautiful erection. It was not that he did not have good ones when he and Monica made love. It was just different down at the bottom of the pool. Sometimes it seemed to him that he was galloping with the satyrs in pursuit of the nymphs. Sometimes he came out of the water and lay on one of the deck chairs and masturbated.

This day as he dove to the bottom, he was not wearing goggles against the chlorine-tainted water. The pool, filled with pure spring water, was perfectly clear in a way the other water in the pool had never been. It was cold. He glided by the nymphs and waited for himself to swell, but nothing happened. Mildly irritated, he blamed his failure on the cold water. He made two other dives with the same result.

When he broke the surface after the third dive, Monica was standing by the steps into the pool. He wondered if she knew about his dives to view the nymphs. He wondered if she had ever watched him lie stretched out on the deck chair with one of those perfect erections.

"You'll have to be careful on days Mrs. Pack is here," she said.

He promised that he would and stepped out of the water. Monica, waiting on the top step, kissed him and put her hand on him. Soon they were lying together on the deck chair. As he moved in her, he looked down at himself. He had a nice erection, but not like in the pool. He wondered if one day he should ask Monica to swim with him among the nymphs and satyrs.

***

He transferred the remaining four carp to the swimming pool. The delivery of the big carp had been delayed. The carp in the pool huddled about the water pump discharge port as if they were confused by the enormous amount of space now available to them. But they eagerly swam across the pool when he patted his hand in the water and fed them food pellets. They nuzzled his hand like eager puppies.

One morning when he came to the pool, he found that they had spread out. One was in the deep end among the nymphs. He decided to swim with them. Mrs. Pack was at work, but he had never seen her come near the pool. And he had no intention of lying down on the deck chair after his swim.

He swam to the deep end and made a dive. He glided by the carp, which paid no attention to him. He imagined what an easy target the fish made for the otters, who were used to pursuing fish like large-mouth bass: a sleek and fast and elusive prey.

Then down there, among the nymphs, he had a magnificent erection. He dived down to the nymphs three times. Then he swam a slow crawl to the shallow end, the drag of the water pleasant against his erection. Luckily for him he stopped his swim and stood up in water that was still more than waist deep. Mrs. Pack was standing by the side of the pool.

"Good morning, Mr. Ferguson," she said.

As he returned her greeting, he was thinking about what she could see of him. He hoped the light was reflecting off the water in such a way that she was blinded. She gave no indication she could. But what did it matter anyway? She had probably seen plenty of naked men in her time.

She immediately went back to dusting the pool furniture. He wondered if Monica had sent her down to the pool on purpose, as a joke. He began to swim laps along the side of the pool as far away from Mrs. Pack as possible. He made a point of not looking toward where she was working. Finally, after he had swum for so long he was exhausted, he paused at the wall of the deep end and looked over at the collection of pool furniture. She was gone.

***

That night he dreamed he and Mrs. Pack, both naked, were swimming laps together. Mrs. Pack's wrinkled face was set atop a perfect body, that of a girl of nineteen or so. He finally realized that they were having some sort of endurance contest. Mrs. Pack never seemed to tire as they swam on and on. Once he looked down and saw that she was swimming on her back just beneath him, using a dolphin kick to propel herself effortlessly though the water. He was at the limit of his endurance. She smiled at him, bubbles trailing from her mouth. He wondered if she were breathing water, like a carp. He was tempted to see if he could too, but was afraid to try.

***

The fish dealer delivered the big carp. It looked bigger than he had expected. This was a fish that should be beyond the reach of any otter. It was the same kind as the last one the otters had eaten, a white fish with a red spot on top of its head. It happened to arrive on one of Mrs. Pack's work days. They all stood by the side of the pool and watched the dealer carefully lower the fish into the pool. The carp swam lazily off toward the deep end.

"Feels right at home," Mrs. Pack observed. "I wonder if it'll eat the little ones."

The dealer laughed.

"All that fish wants to eat is food pellets. He'll take'em right out of your hand."

Mrs. Pack went off to her work. He wondered if Monica had told her how much she had paid for the fish. He was sure that Mrs. Pack would have been shocked if she learned the price. The dealer lingered for a time over coffee Monica brought out to the pool. Then he left.

"I could raise plenty of fish in this pool," Monica said.

"I thought you were going to raise horses," he said.

She pointed out that the barn needed to be put in good order.

"It was hard enough getting the renovations on the house done," she said.

He wondered if Monica was happy with the sort of life they were living. She seemed to be. Sometimes he wondered if she was sorry they had not had children.

46

"Now that the fish are safe you can start on your studio," she said.

"Maybe after the barn."

"No, the barn can wait."

He wondered how he would feel when the studio was completed. Then he would have to paint. Perhaps he would take some classes in Memphis first and see if he could do something that showed some talent.

For a moment he considered asking her if she were happy, if this place was where she wanted to spend the rest of her life. He looked out at the pool, soon to be full of carp. Once it was filled with damaged children. For a time he had used it as a theatre to act out his sexual fantasies. Now the brightly-colored carp would swim in schools among the nymphs. When the pool became that crowded, he did not think he would care to swim there any longer.

No, she was obviously quite content with the property. She would think, and rightly so, that his asking was a way of telling her that he was not satisfied. He resolved that he would draw up some plans and consult an architect in Memphis about the best way to install a studio in the deserted wing.

***

The next week he was in his office working on plans for the studio when he heard Monica calling his name. Then her footsteps as she ran through the house and burst into his office.

"Those damn otters ate my fish," she shouted. "I want them dead! I want them dead, dead, dead!"

"Not the new fish?"

"No, Lady Shonagon and Prince Kaoru."

She still had not yet decided upon a name for the new fish. If she filled the pool with fish, she would probably have to abandon the practice of giving them names.

He left Monica in the house and went to the pool where he found the place where the otters had chewed a hole in the screen. There was blood next to the pool and a piece of a fin. The otters had eaten their fill and then carried the rest away to their young. He cleaned up the blood and pieces of fish. The remaining fish were in a tight group next to the filter port. The new fish was at the bottom of the deep end.

Monica wanted the otters dead. But even if he killed them all, new ones would move in. And although he had been caught up in the hunt for them (it was always a disappointment to find one of the humane traps empty), he really had no interest in killing them. He thought of the methods: poison, dynamite dropped into their den, a rifleman armed with night vision equipment. The rifleman was how his golf club had dealt with an overpopulation of deer. They did it at night with rifles equipped with silencers.

He fed the remaining carp some food pellets to take their minds off the raid by the otters. The new fish remained at the bottom of the deep end. He threw some pellets into the water there, knowing eventually they would sink down to him. The fish did not rise to take them.

He then spent the rest of the day nailing up pieces of plywood over the lower part of the screen. The next day he planned to make a trip to a building supply store in the suburbs of Memphis to buy wire mesh to replace the plywood. That would surely bring an end to their problems with the otters.

***

He was using a pneumatic stapler to attach the wire mesh when he saw Mrs. Pack walking across the lawn. It was hot work. There was no shade, and he had not started until after lunch. Mrs. Pack carried a glass of iced tea in one hand and a pitcher in the other. Monica must have sent her.

48

He thanked her for the tea and put the pitcher in a patch of shade. He took a drink as Mrs. Pack stood before him and shaded her eyes against the glare and watched him. It was sweet tea. Neither he or Monica drank that. But it was cold, and it was easy to give Mrs. Pack the impression it was exactly what he wanted. He thanked her. She told him that Monica was gone when she arrived. She had probably gone to the grocery store. So it must have been Mrs. Pack's idea to bring the tea to him.

She stepped up to the wire mesh and ran her fingers over it.

"Won't be able to chew through that," she said.

Then she looked at the expanse of screen above the mesh.

"They won't climb that high," he said.

"You sure?" she asked.

He said he was but realized as he said it that he had no idea how well otters could climb.

"They're hungry," she said.

He said nothing in reply and drained the glass. The ice was melting fast; the tea tasted thin and sickeningly sweet.

"Dead otters won't eat your wife's fish," she said. "Be a shame to lose expensive fish like that."

He again wondered if Monica had told her how much she had paid for the big carp. He noticed she was not sweating. How was that possible?

"You let me talk to my cousin," she said.

He glanced at the expanse of uncovered screen and told her he would appreciate it if she asked him to deal with the otters.

"You won't be sorry," she said.

Then she went back to the house. He returned to his work.

***

Monica was pleased when he told her that Mrs. Pack's cousin had agreed to help. But when the day arrived for the extermination of the otters the cousin's son showed up instead.

"Daddy says he's real busy," the boy said.

He had brought his father's feist, a squirrel dog, with him. The little dog was trembling with excitement. Sam knew about squirrel dogs, which were trained to tree squirrels. The boy was disappointed that his father had sent him with the dog. He was home on leave after his third tour in Iraq. He was a demolition man and was eager to dynamite the otters' den. But his father had forbidden him to use it.

"That'll solve your problem," the boy said. "Get 'em all, big ones and little ones."

Sam considered telling the boy to go home, that he would install mesh over the rest of the screen. But then Monica came out to meet the boy and cooed over the dog and told the boy, his name was Michael, that they both would be forever in his debt if he could rid them of the otters. She told the boy about Sam's efforts with the humane traps.

"Traps," the boy said. "Not worth much. But you couldn't have known that. It's not your fault."

They walked through the fields to the river. The otters had dug a burrow among the roots of a huge poplar. The plan was to send the feist into the den and drive out the otters. Then Michael would shoot them with the shotgun he carried, barrel down, on a sling over his shoulder.

Michael released the feist, whose name was Elmo, at the opening of the burrow. Elmo ran in circles and sniffed eagerly at the opening. Then he darted off into the trees. Soon they heard him yelping.

"Found him a squirrel," Michael said. "Too bad it's not squirrel season."

They located the dog. He had his front paws up on the trunk of the tree, his head thrown back, and was yapping furiously. The dog seemed indignant that Michael did not take up the shotgun. The boy picked up Elmo, squirming and whining in protest, and carried him back to the burrow. He nosed around the opening and then ran off into the trees again.

Michael was patient. He never got mad at the dog but brought him back three times to the entrance of the burrow. He speculated that maybe the otters and their young were in the river. But he admitted that Elmo should have gone eagerly into the burrow.

"Wouldn't matter to him if there was a wild hog in there," Michael said. "It ain't that he's afraid."

Sam was quick to point out he had no doubts about the dog's courage.

Then Michael offered to come back with dynamite. He promised certain results. But Sam decided that he would go ahead and put up the screen. He expected it would take several days. He was not eager to spend more time in the hot sun up on a ladder. But he found he was thankful the feist had failed. He had not been looking forward to seeing Michael shoot the otters as the feist drove them out of the den.

When they returned to the house, he was pleased to see that Monica's car was gone. He did not want to give Michael the opportunity to make his dynamite speech to Monica. She was out for blood. She had no sympathy for the otters, young or old.

***

He and Monica lay in bed. She was reading an article about carp. He was thinking about how nice it would be to spend the rest of the evening making love. He leaned over and nuzzled the nearest breast. Monica giggled.

"Do you know Mrs. Pack's name is Audrey?" she said. "I wouldn't have expected that. It doesn't seem to fit her, a name like that. She's a Hillwright. Her people live out in the country near

Water Valley."

As she spoke she put down her magazine and turned toward him. He wrapped his arms about her. Usually he would now let himself be caught up in the delicious flow of the lovemaking. And things proceeded as usual but instead of reveling in the feel of nipple and thigh, of her hands on him, he was thinking instead of Mrs. Pack. And not really of her but of a girl named Audrey Hillwright.

His college roommate Tom had a male friend named Beverly. He seemed to recall that Beverly was from Virginia. Beverly had told Tom that he was going out with a girl who would, on request, fuck all of them. Those were the words he heard coming out of Tom's mouth. It was the sixties and things like that were not exactly uncommon. He expected she was some hippie girl. He still wore his hair short and drank whiskey instead of smoking marijuana. He was a virgin, a secret he guarded closely, and the opportunity to lose his virginity was something that he thought about constantly.

That night they met Beverly and the girl at Beverly's apartment. It was one of those tiny student apartments with a single bedroom. The girl was not the hippie he expected. She had not dropped out of the university. She had graduated from the county high school and was working as a telephone operator. Now, no matter how hard he tried, he could not imagine how her metamorphosis into Mrs. Pack had occurred.

They all sat around and drank beer a while and listened to music. Then Beverly took the girl into the bedroom and shut the door. Tom took up a pornographic book and began to read. They were both concerned about maintaining an erection. Tom claimed that pornography always did the trick for him. Sam had never talked to anyone about maintaining an erection. He admired the way Tom did it so casually.

Beverly came out of the bedroom. He looked bored as if he had already grown weary of the girl. It was Tom's turn. They had flipped a coin. Tom disappeared into the bedroom. Sam started to take up the book.

"You won't need that," Beverly said. "Let's see what he's doing."

They went outside and around to the bedroom window. The light was on and they looked through a crack in the blinds. Sam saw the girl putting her hand on Tom's erection. She released him and his cock bobbed up and down. He lowered himself on top of her. She was smiling. He looked away from the window, feeling guilty at being a voyeur at his friend's private moment. But Beverly remained at the window. Then he too turned away.

"Sam," Monica murmured.

He was inside her and, intimately acquainted with each other's bodies, they moved in accustomed rhythms. He was there with her and in the bedroom with the girl at the same time, for after Tom emerged, a smile on his face, he had taken his turn.

He had been clumsy. She lay there available and smiling. But he remained limp in her hands as she stroked him.

"Do that with a little more authority," he said.

She laughed and did as he asked. He felt himself swell, and he came into her.

Those had been his words, that formal statement. She had told Beverly and Tom what he had said. For months afterwards when they smoked marijuana together, Audrey Hillwright long gone from their lives, someone would bring up his statement and everyone at the party would laugh that shrill, foolish laughter of the stoned.

Monica moaned and murmured something he could not understand. She was close to the end, but he felt himself shrinking. Then she was there, and she writhed beneath him in a way he always found exciting. But this time instead of excitement he felt only despair. He could not remember exactly how Mrs. Pack had felt beneath him when she was not Mrs. Pack but that young girl, no older than he, named Audrey.

He rolled off Monica who immediately snuggled up against him, her head on his chest.

"Are you all right?" she asked.

He was covered in sweat although the air-conditioning was turned down low, the room cold, just the way Monica liked it.

"Fine," he said. "Fine."

She began to talk about her plans for raising carp. He was thankful she was no longer on the subject of Mrs. Pack.

But he still felt uncomfortable. He forced himself to take deep, slow, even breaths. He tried to think of the most pleasant and calming thing possible. So he thought of himself swimming in the pool among the nymphs. But suddenly, as he felt his body begin to relax and the beautiful images fill his mind, Mrs. Pack glided by, and he found himself breathing water and knew with certainty he would drown.

Rocks

I'VE always suspected that my grandfather never really liked my father, his only son, and I know he liked the woman he married even less. So when my mother got eaten by a lion in Africa I suppose my grandfather was secretly pleased. They never found her body, only her Vassar t-shirt. One time when my grandfather and I were fishing together he said it was a smart lion because a shirt from a school like that was likely to give a lion a bad case of indigestion. My grandfather was a little drunk at the time. I don't think he really had a clear idea where that school was, only that it was in the North some place and they didn't have a football team. Thinking about my mother dying in Africa made me start to cry. I must have been about nine or ten at the time. I suppose he was sorry he said it, but he said things like that pretty often when he was drinking. And that was most of the time. As far as he was concerned a trout stream was just as good a place as any. You wouldn't think a man with that much whiskey in him could put a trout fly into some of the places he did, but I was there to witness those magical casts. To make up for what he said he let me have a drink of whiskey out of his silver flask and promised me a new fly rod for Christmas.

Lately, now that I'm about to go off to college, I've realized that my mother was probably the only person in the history of that school who became a Baptist missionary.

I was lucky I wasn't eaten too. They found me lying on the ground in the bush. They never found any trace of my mother, although I suppose they looked hard. One lion in Africa looks pretty much like another so what are you going to do? Kill them all and go digging about for my mother's remains in each one? My grandfather always hinted that my father knew more about my mother's death than he was willing to say. But when I'd ask my father he'd just say that he'd told me all he knew. That it was a mystery to him too.

Now my grandfather is dead. I'd always hoped he'd decide to forgive my father for marrying my mother, who turned my father into a missionary. My grandfather didn't believe in any sort of god, certainly not that Christian god. My father said a prayer at his burial which would have made my grandfather mad if he'd been alive to hear it. What made my grandfather madder than the Christian stuff was my father's "hippie ways." I can hear my grandfather saying that. It was one of his favorite expressions when I was around him. My father believes in things like reincarnation. He believes in Jesus too. After my mother's death he shifted pieces of various religions around until he got himself one that suited him. He says he's still a Baptist, but I've never seen him go to church. He lets me believe whatever I want. I've never been baptized. The neighbors let both of us know what they think of that every time they get a chance. Let's see. How would I describe my father to someone who's never met him? Well, he grows vegetables in an organic garden. He built our house. I helped. He's made a good living as a potter. His work has won prizes. His work sells. But he did give up being a missionary. Africa cured him. He never got over my mother's death. I can't recall another woman ever being in our house.

When my grandfather's will was read, I discovered he had not forgiven my father. In his will he left all his land to my father's brother Jack, and he left all the rocks in the creek that runs behind the house my father built to me. I'm supposed dig them out with my uncle Jack's track cat and sell them in Charlotte. Folks use them for landscaping. Then I'm supposed to buy myself a nice SUV. It lays it all out right there in the will. All this, of course, is calculated to drive my father wild. He ponders for months over the cutting of a single tree. That creek is one of his favorite places. He'll sit on this particular rock at the foot of a little waterfall for hours and smoke marijuana and think about things. I try to stay clear of both: marijuana and too much thinking. My grandfather has been dead three years and I've just turned eighteen, the age stipulated in the will for me to start hauling rocks.

Uncle Jack has been encouraging me to go ahead and do it. He was also not fond of my mother and is just as critical as the neighbors about the way my father has conducted his life. I know how to operate a track cat. I learned when I was thirteen from Uncle Jack and have been working for him every summer to save money for college. There's a part of me that just wants to leave those rocks alone. But Uncle Jack keeps pointing out nice SUVs to me, and I think about how good my kayak and mountain bike will look on one of those and how I'll find some girl at Chapel Hill who likes to bike and kayak and we can go off on weekend trips together. We could put a double air mattress in the back and sleep better than if we'd stayed at a hotel. After all they're *my* rocks. It says it right there in the will. And I'll have to work hard digging them out. I calculate that I'll have to move maybe one-hundred to two-hundred tons of rocks. Maybe more. Some especially nice boulders might go for two or three thousand dollars if you bought them from the landscape people in Charlotte. I'll get a lot less.

Ever since graduation I've been turning the idea of that SUV over and over in my mind. Finally now, in the middle of July, I give in to it. It's the perfect time to dig rocks. We haven't had rain for weeks. The creek is so low that the trout are in danger of getting sunburned. I'll have to work hard though if I expect to get them out of there and down to Charlotte and sold before I go off to the university. So I talk with Uncle Jack about it and he says that it's ok for me to use the track cat as long as I want and his truck and flatbed trailer to haul them to Charlotte. He has a crane I can use to load them onto the trailer. Uncle Jack has made a good living as a heavy equipment contractor. He sells and services it too.

I tell my father over breakfast.

"They're your rocks," he says.

"My truck is pretty well finished," I say.

"I know."

I wish he'd get mad or something and not be so resigned to it. Laconic is a word you could use to describe him. I know words like that because I've read all my father's books and most in the library in town. That's why I did so well on the SAT and won a scholarship. I think of his favorite place by the water and decide that I'm going to leave those rocks and especially his favorite rock alone.

"You'll have to make some roads down to the creek," he says.

"I'll seed fescue over 'em so they won't wash," I say. "In a couple of years you won't even be able to tell they were there."

Both of us know that's not true. The marks of those roads will be there for a long time, maybe even after we're both dead.

Uncle Jack takes great care not to let silt get into the streams. He's a trout fisherman. He cares about the streams just as much as my father. Only he's not a catch and release man, and he and my father have had words about that.

"I know," he said. "Jack's good about that. He taught you well."

And I'm thinking that I should just forget about those rocks. My truck needs some work, but I can do most of that in Jack's shop. It's my father not getting mad that makes me madder than if he had, so I decide that I'll do it.

"In a couple of years you'll never know I've been in there," I

58

say.

That's partially true. The rhododendrons will grow quickly and the winter and spring rains will rearrange anything that's left loose down in the creek bed.

"I'll know," he says.

That's the end of our conversation. He goes off to his studio to throw a pot.

***

I'm not going to try to take the track cat through the whole creek. I'll concentrate on a stretch that's relatively flat. All along are dense rhododendron thickets, and I'll use the claw to cut a path through them down to the water. I've got my eye on five or six good-sized boulders that would look great in those rich people's gardens in Charlotte. I'll bring them back up to the road. When I get enough, I'll load 'em onto the flat bed trailer, lash 'em on tight with chains and steel cables, and drive the load down to Charlotte.

As I pull up the first boulder, which fits easily into the claw, I work the controls to lift it out. The boulder resists for a moment or two, and the frame of the cat track shudders from the strain. Then after all those millions of years of lying there it gives up and I pull it free, pieces of roots and forest debris falling as I lift it into the air. I imagine there must have been a sucking sound as the claw tore it out of the ground, but of course I can't hear that over the sound of the engine.

"Why didn't that lion eat me?" I say.

"I don't know," I say.

I sometimes have these conversations with myself while I work. And almost always they are about how I survived out there in the bush.

My father knows the answer. Jesus protected me. I lay out there in the bush for three or four hours before my father and the others found me. Later the tracker said that there were the fresh prints of a big lioness all around me. How did that tracker know that? I mean how did he know it was a lioness? I sure would like to talk with him. He could be the solver of mysteries for me. I wonder if he could tell that the lion that made the tracks was the one that ate my mother? But that country has been at war off and on for years now, and I wouldn't be surprised if he were dead.

I've never got a clear explanation from my father about what my mother was doing out there with me. Perhaps she went out there alone to pray. I'm fairly certain that she didn't plan on being eaten by a lion. But you never know about Christians. Over the centuries they've seemed pretty eager for various forms of violent death.

Sometimes I try to imagine what went through my mind as I lay there. Did I see vultures circling overhead? Most likely all I saw were the colors of the sky and clouds and the sun coming through the branches of the acacia I lay under. It was lucky I was in the shade. That equatorial sun would have fried me. A few ants or beetles could've crawled over me. Maybe a spider. I don't like to think about snakes. Yes, I could've smelled the dust. It was the dry season. Maybe that big lioness sniffed at me. I guess I would've smelled of my mother's milk, feces, urine. Baby smells.

Thinking this is nothing new to me. It's like a daydream I've learned by rote. Sometimes I say the whole thing out loud, my words lost in the noise of the engine.

I back up the track cat, moving slowly to give the tracks an opportunity to get a good grip and the weight of the boulder in the claw making it sway a little in a way I don't like. I continue talking, but this time I have the conversation with my mother. My questions and her responses never vary. It's like we're performing a play. I've never written down the words. What would be the point of that?

I imagine her standing there. She's just like the picture in my father's bedroom. Once she looked old, but now she looks just like those girls in my graduating class. We're always in Africa. The plain stretches away all around us, and there is a herd of some sort of animals off in the distance, but they're too far away for me to identify them.

"What were you doing out there?" I ask.

"Looking for Jesus," she says.

"Jesus was never in Africa."

"He's everywhere?"

It's one of those insane conversations you can have with religions people if you're foolish enough to have them. Their talk goes round and round and off to nowhere.

"Why did you take me with you?" I ask.

"To see Jesus," she says.

Then I have to listen to the "suffer the little children" stuff. It's gotten so that I don't even bother to listen to that part of our conversation in my imagination.

"Yes, I know," I say. "But did you put me down and go mistake a lion for Jesus?"

Here I, my character, young or old, whoever I am in my imagination, laughs. But she doesn't.

"I don't make mistakes about Jesus," she says. "I *know*."

"Show me what happened," I say. "I want to *see*."

I can't or won't imagine what happens. Who would want to imagine in detail their mother getting eaten by a lion?

I drop the rock by the road. I know that my father can hear the sound of the engine in his studio. Or maybe he's decided to go into town on the days that I work. I've estimated that three weeks should be enough for me to collect enough rocks to buy an SUV, particularly if I'm careful and choose interesting ones, those with lichen and moss still on them or with holes scoured out by the creek at high water as the force of the water rattled pebbles around in a crevice. People won't pay much for something that's been blasted out of a quarry, the sides of the boulder all raw and jagged. They want their rocks with the look and smell of age on them, rounded slowly over millions of years by the action of the stream.

I have a good day. By late in the afternoon there are six good boulders awaiting the crane.

When I get back to the house, I discover a note from my father. He's going to spend a few days with some friends at Black Mountain. He doesn't say so in the note, but I suppose he just can't bear to see me giving in to his father's wishes and destroying the creek. And I think to myself what does it matter. One day those rocks will be at the bottom of the sea or at the top of a mountain range higher the Himalayas or changed into molten lava. And it's likely there won't be a single human being around to look at any of it.

With him gone I have to cook for myself. My father is a great cook. He puts all those vegetables we grow to good use. He buys his meat from local farmers, and we usually shoot a couple of deer every year.

I make myself some venison tacos with tomatoes and lettuce from our garden. I drink a beer. I'm allowed one a day and it's an agreement I've never broken. Then I go sit out on the screened porch. It's almost dark and bats are twisting in the air above the garden. I hear my father's waterfall at the bottom of the hill below the house. If I dug out a few choice boulders from the pool below, would the rush of the water sound different? Could he tell without even looking at it, just by the sound? That hardly seems possible but you never know with my father.

It's a warm night so I go to sleep on the cot on the screened porch with the sound of the creek in my ears. I hope to dream of Africa.

***

After three days I've lifted enough rocks out of the creek to make a load to take to Charlotte. Uncle Jack comes out with a crane and helps me lift them onto the trailer. We can't get as many on it as I'd hoped, but finally we have them all tied down and ready for the trip. My father has still not returned.

I hook the truck up to the trailer and drive over to the interstate and go down the mountain to Charlotte.

I think of my dream of Africa, the one I wish I'd have again but haven't had lately. I'm an infant lying on the ground beneath that acacia tree. I look up and laugh at the play of light and shadows as a breeze stirs the branches. Then I realize there're lions about. So I climb right up that tree just like a squirrel. The lions fill the space below. There are hundreds of them. They don't snarl or try to climb up the tree. They just lie there in the dust. They are the color of the dust. I smell of the stink of them. I climb higher and higher until I'm at the very top, and I can't understand how the thin branches can bear my weight. I begin to wonder if I'm flying. Way off across the plain I can see a river and herds of animals, and maybe there's a figure that's my mother walking toward that piece of blue amid the brown plain. But everything shimmers in the heat and I can't be sure and the figure disappears.

Thinking about the dream is disappointing, not the same as having it. So I give up on African dreams and start thinking about the girl I haven't met yet who's going kayaking with me in my new SUV.

At the landscaper's I watch them unload the rocks. I've weighed them at the truck scales on the interstate and know we have a little over twenty tons. But the price will also depend on the individual character of the boulders. I've dragged some good ones out of the creek. I end up with almost two-thousand dollars. That's pure profit. Uncle Jack has said he won't charge me for the use of equipment or diesel.

Gradually the money in my bank account accumulates. Everyone at the bank knows about me selling the rocks. Some probably disapprove but nobody ever says anything about it.

Then my father comes home from Black Mountain. I wonder if he's gotten reports from the neighbors about the progress I've made. It seems to me that if I were him, I'd have waited until I finished. If he goes to the creek to look, he never says anything to me about it. He spends most of the time in his studio. He begins to work at night and sleep doing the day, something he's never done before. We hardly see each other. I take a day off now and then to make sure the garden is weeded.

Just about the time I take my last load down to Charlotte, he stops working at night. He starts spending time down at the waterfall. That's not unusual. He often does that after he's finished a project. As he sits there for hours, he probably thinks about the next one or maybe he just wants to clear the one he's just finished out of his mind.

I wonder if he's thinking of Africa, playing over and over in his mind that something he's concealed from me all these years. I've considered the possibility that my grandfather invented that as a way to get back at my father just like he thought up the idea of leaving me the rocks in his will. Maybe he just can't acknowledge that at that time years ago in Africa my mother was a little crazy. After all, a certain percentage of women kill their babies. But she didn't kill me. She wasn't that sort of crazy.

I think hard about her as I sit on the screened porch while my father is down at his waterfall sitting on his rock and most likely thinking of her. I can imagine the puffs of dust beneath her feet as she walks through the bush carrying me while somewhere out there in the tall grass a lioness is watching.

I close my eyes and try to smell her sweat, feel the impact of her feet on the rough ground travel up her body and into mine. Her breasts must have been full of milk. Was she nursing me as she walked? Or was I asleep and when I opened my eyes she was gone and I was lying under the acacia, those patterns of light and darkness flickering across my face.

It's clear to me I can go no further. But I've gotten used to the failure of my imagination. I'm not going to try to imagine her death. I've never done that. I just want to know what she was doing out there. Jesus as a lion. Jesus as violent death. That's where I always end up, and I know she didn't imagine that.

***

I spend some time trying to decide what sort of SUV to buy and finally settle on a Land Rover. Does Africa have something to do with my choice? I'm not sure. There's a dealership out on the highway. They sell to the rich people who have come to the mountains to retire. After I negotiate a deal with the salesman, who won't back off much on the price, I go to the bank and withdraw enough to pay for it.

Driving it home is the hard part. I expect to have words with my father. But he refuses to acknowledge its existence, doesn't say a word at lunch or at supper.

When I get up in the morning, I see him out in the driveway with a cup of coffee in his hand. He slowly walks around it. Then he comes into the house.

"You know that you are a pawn in the hands of that old man," he says. "I never though he could cause so much grief after he was dead. At least it's over now."

"I'm sorry about the creek," I say.

It's true. At that moment I wish I could put every rock back.

"I don't care about the creek," he says.

"Yes, you do," I say. "What if I took your favorite rock out of the waterfall pool? Would you care about that?"

The track cat is parked just above the pool. I imagine cutting a path down through the rhododendrons and ripping out that rock. My father would have to find another place to get high. As I think of doing it, it's just like someone has send a bolt of electricity through my body.

"I care about you," my father says.

"He said you know about my mother," I say.

"We've had this conversation before."

"What do you know that you haven't told me?"

"All I know is that he and Jack didn't like your mother. She believed in what she was doing."

"Did you?"

"At the time I did."

He pours me a cup of coffee and hands it to me. I wrap my hands around the mug. It's one he made. It the sort of mug that's perfectly balanced, that feels good in my hands.

"Let's go down to the creek," he says.

I don't really want to go there. I don't want to watch him look at what I've done. I've destroyed something he loves, and all I've gotten out of it is something that in ten years or so will be sold for scrap.

"To the waterfall," he says.

I agree to that. I'm glad that I haven't touched it. He can sit there and pretend that the rest of the creek is exactly the same.

We walk down to the creek and both take a seat on his rock. I run my hands over it and shudder at the thought of lowering the claw of the track cat down on it. He lights a joint.

"I've nothing to add to what I've already told you," he says. "You can't know everything. No one will ever know what went on out there."

I think of my grandfather's words. I think of the taste of the whisky from his flask. Then I ask him if he believes that Jesus saved me, and he gives me the same answer he always does.

"Then there's no mystery about me," I say.

I've tried this sort of indirection before. He supposed to fill in the blank space.

"It was meant to be," he says.

That's the answer I always receive. It tells me nothing.

And now the thought of ripping that rock out with the track cat is a pleasant one.

"So she was out in the bush looking for Jesus or something like that?" I say.

He shrugs his shoulders.

"Could be," he says. "But that's not the answer you want. Just let the mystery of it be."

I suspect that he may be right about my grandfather. I've been a fool. Jack is laughing. My grandfather laughed when he thought up the terms of the will. But the rocks are gone. Maybe they'll give some pleasure to the people who bought them.

Then we just sit there, the rush of the water all around us. I smell the water, the mud, the fragrant stink of my father's joint. Neither of us says anything. I try to understand how I feel. Finally I decide it's like getting momentarily pinned in a kayak against a rock or log. That's happened to me before. I'm upside down and holding my breath while I look up at the blue sky through that perfectly clear water and work myself out of the pin. And then I roll up and take in great gulps of fresh air. I begin to think that life for me is going to be as if I'm never able to roll up and I'm there, trapped, struggling, waiting for my last breath of air to run out.

Lovers of Hurricanes

ALL summer Constantine watched the corn grow. Viewed from the deck of the cabin, which lay between the river and the field, it looked much like a green sea, especially when the wind moved across the stalks, making a sound like his favorite trout stream. Because it was being irrigated with water drawn from the river, it grew tall and rich and green in the midst of a rainless summer. The rattle of the pump and the pulse of the giant sprinklers had become as much a part of the sounds of summer as the cicadas in the live oaks or the cooing of the nesting mourning doves in the evening. Now it was late September and the corn was ready to be harvested.

This part of South Carolina, the beginning of the low country some sixty miles from the sea, had been caught in the grip of a drought for several years, so that some people had begun to hope a hurricane would again come this way. There was still downed timber in the woods from where the last one had moved through, but the terror and misery brought by the storm had been forgotten, replaced by the need for water. People were losing their land to the drought.

Last summer when he and his wife Clarissa made love on the screened porch a breeze would sometimes catch up the water from one of the sprinklers and carry it against the screen to fall as a fine mist on their sweat-covered bodies. But it did not smell like rain.

There was the scent of rubber and the taste of metal in the water.

Clarissa died in August of breast cancer, three years after she had undergone a double mastectomy. He discovered living as he had lived before was impossible. He went to work every day at his land surveying business and came home at night to an empty house. One day as he was standing in a soybean field making a calculation, he realized this sort of work was not going to save him from the despair that was becoming an all- too familiar companion.

So six months after Clarissa's death he shut down his land surveying business to become a wildlife photographer, something he had wanted to do ever since he had taken a photography course in college.

To give himself money to live on he had sold the house and the attached farmland to a retired banker from New Hampshire.

The house, marked by its twin brick chimneys, lay beyond the slough that bordered the eastern end of the cornfield. The house had been built by one of his ancestors, the earliest settler in the county, on land only slightly higher than the slough. It was protected from flooding by a system of private levees.

He converted the land surveying office into a studio and went to live at the cabin. Built as a hunting shack not long after the Civil War, it had been rebuilt a number of times after the river flooded and carried it away. But the pilings he set it on fifteen years before, after it was washed away by high water, were tall enough to keep it out of reach of the river, which would simply spread out across the field after it had reached a certain level. The pilings lifted the cabin above the tops of small trees like dogwoods and redbuds and placed it among the second story of the live oaks and gums. He liked the feeling. It was as if he were in a tree house.

Clarissa had never been fond of the cabin, visiting it only a few times in their long marriage. It was not filled with memories of her as the house had been. He knew he would always have her in his mind, but now that he had changed the direction of his life he thought her death was a loss he could more easily accept. Yet he still sometimes expected to wake up in the morning and find her in bed with him, even in the cabin where she had only spend the night twice.

He devoted his time to roaming the land along the river, which he still owned, and photographing the pair of eagles that had built a nest high in a big cypress. One day he came upon a pair of rattlesnakes performing a mating dance, the big rattlers reared up like cobras. He sold that picture and the story he wrote to go with it to a magazine. After he stumbled upon a ribbon snake giving birth and took a series of pictures that turned out well, he started thinking he might specialize in snakes.

***

The first tropical depression of the season appeared off the coast of Africa, a clump of clouds on his computer screen. In a few days it organized itself as the first hurricane of the season, bearing the name of Anne. A few days later Anne became a powerful storm at mid-Atlantic, bearing down on the eastern tip of Cuba. The forecasters were predicting it would make landfall in the United States, somewhere between the Carolinas and Jacksonville.

They were cutting the corn in the field next to the cabin. They had been cutting since early in the morning. There was not a cloud in the sky, no hint a hurricane was prowling about in the Atlantic. The scent of dust and corn and cut silage hung in the air. The picker poured a gold stream of kernels into the truck that followed behind it, and the stripped cobs were spit back to lie in heaps in the field.

He lay in a hammock drinking a beer while he watched the picker move past the cabin. It was no more than fifty yards away, for the cornfield came right up to the edge of his yard. Then he heard a sort of clang as if someone had dropped a hammer onto a metal floor. The picker stopped and the operator climbed out of it. He was joined by the man driving the truck that received the corn. They walked around the picker a few times and peered into the machinery. One of them took out a cell phone.

Soon Constantine saw a truck coming across the field. A woman dressed in jeans and work boots got out and talked with them. They all walked around the picker. She took a toolbox out of the pickup. She removed an access panel and put her head down into the machinery. Once she had one of them hold a flashlight for her. Then she withdrew herself from the machinery and replaced the panel. The operator climbed up on the picker and started the engine. The picker and the truck moved off while she stood beside her truck, wiping grease off her hands with a paper towel.

She looked toward the cabin for the first time, and he raised his bottle of beer to her.

"Come and have a beer," he shouted.

She hesitated for a moment. Then she nodded her head.

She disappeared into the corn and emerged into his yard. She came up the steps.

"I'm covered with grease," she said.

It was just her hands that were dirty. He realized that was why she had accepted his offer, a chance to wash her hands.

After she scrubbed her hands at the kitchen sink, they sat together on the porch. Her name was Madeline Bryan. She was the owner of the custom cutting company, which she and her husband, now dead, had started. Like everyone in Bishopville, she knew about Clarissa's death and his sale of the house. He discovered she was from a small town in the Mississippi Delta where her father, who had recently died, had been a pharmacist. She had gone to the state engineering university where she took a degree in civil engineering. The jeans she wore were not just something convenient to work in.

They fit her too well for that. She expected men to look at her and like what they saw.

"That's good land," she said. "I could get over selling the house but not the land."

"My kin are mad about the house," he said. "I never really farmed the land. I just rented it out."

"Then you've never been a farmer?"

"No."

"I haven't either. I've just done the cutting. But I worry about the drought just like they do."

"You could move. Go cut in Texas if you wish. They can't."

"Yes, that's true."

He wished he had not implied she could afford to be indifferent to the drought. He considered making an apology but decided to say nothing.

She turned and looked out over the field.

"Maybe you miss owning this land more than you know," she said. She looked up at the sky. It was late afternoon and the air over the cabin was filled with chimney swifts. "That hurricane comes up this way and I won't be able to cut for a couple of weeks. I'm cutting at night just in case. But my crew has to sleep some time."

He invited her for dinner on Friday. She accepted but warned him she might have to leave unexpectedly if a cutter broke down.

***

The hurricane swung past Cuba without making landfall and then headed straight for the Carolinas. He watched it on the TV as he prepared dinner. He was cooking doves in a white wine sauce. He had shot them that afternoon. The cut cornfield was full of them, the birds coming in to feed on the spilled grain. He sautéed them in a pan with olive oil and then put them in the cast iron pot with the wine sauce to slowly cook in the oven. They would have tomatoes and eggplant from his garden and jasmine rice.

She arrived dressed in shorts, sandals, and a blue cotton top. He put on a CD.

"Do you like jazz?" he asked.

"Yes," she said.

And she began to tell him about listening to jazz in Charleston and New Orleans.

As they ate he kept expecting her pager was going to beep, but it did not. He was hoping she would spend the night with him.

After dinner they sat on the porch and listened to one CD after another.

"Would you like to dance?" he asked.

"Later," she said. "Let's look at the hurricane."

They went inside and he turned on the TV. Anne was moving straight for South Carolina. Great swirls of clouds stretched northward. The eye was tight and well defined, an especially powerful storm. In two days the leading edge of it would reach the South Carolina coast.

She told him how she and her husband liked to get as close to hurricanes as possible. It was hard for them to travel because the harvesting season was during hurricane season. But when hurricanes came close to South Carolina and the rain shut down the harvesting they would get in the car and drive to the coast. They would take a hotel room somewhere in the projected path of the storm.

"Then what would you do?" he asked.

"Wait, watch it on TV," she said. "Sometimes we'd be evacuated but other times we got to stay."

She walked to the window and looked out into the trees.

"Could this cabin survive a hurricane?" she asked.

He explained the typography of the river basin, how the water would simply spread out across the fields. And as he was talking about hundred year high water levels, he wondered what it would be like to be with her in the cabin during a big storm.

"We may get a little of Anne," he said. "We could come out here. It wouldn't the same as being on the coast."

"Oh, I wouldn't want to do *that* again," she said.

She told him she expected to harvest for two more days. He would pick her up at her house.

"What about your truck?" she asked.

"We'll leave it on high ground and ride bicycles," he said.

"What if the cabin starts to wash away?"

"We'll moor my bass boat there."

"Power?"

"I've got a generator. We'll watch the storm on TV and eat steaks."

"You've thought of everything. Were you thinking about asking me to sit out the storm with you when you invited me for a beer?"

"If you hadn't needed to wash your hands you wouldn't have come."

"Probably not."

After she left he watched the storm on TV. It was going to rain hard, and the river would flood. He did not expect much wind, not this far inland. The prediction was for the storm to track up the coast and then out to sea, where it would die in the cooler water of the North Atlantic.

As he went to sleep that night, he imagined her and her husband making love in hotel rooms in the glow of the light from the TV or in the dark because the power had gone out. Her husband had been dead for three years. He supposed if he got to know her better she might tell him exactly how she had managed to live her life without him. They had run the company together, both of the them in the field with the machines. She must be thinking of him constantly as she went about the duties they had once shared.

He spent the next two days making the cabin ready for the flood. As he worked the image of himself in bed with her while the rain pounded on the metal roof of the cabin was constantly in his mind.

***

When late in the afternoon they rode bicycles to the cabin, first going down the highway to the river bottom below and then on gravel roads through the fields, the sky was overcast but no rain was falling yet. Anne was bearing down upon the coast just north of Charleston.

He had the sensation of being a boy again, of riding his bike in aimless patterns on gravel roads. The feeling was even stronger when they left the gravel road for the dirt one that led to the cabin. The dirt, reduced to a fine dust by weeks of no rain, hissed beneath the tires of his bike. And he was taken back to a summer morning when as a boy he had ridden this same dirt track to the cabin.

They took the bicycles up the steps. The first thing they did was turn the TV to the weather channel. The hurricane was still on course, the eye sixty miles offshore. Heavy rain was expected to reach them around midnight.

He went about checking his preparations while she prepared supper. He had offered to cook, but she insisted she wanted to make stuffed flounder according to a recipe she had learned from her grandmother in Biloxi. He had parked the bass boat on its trailer on the downstream side of the porch steps. The rising water would float it off the trailer. He lashed its cover down tightly to keep it from filling up with water. He was sure they would not be forced into the boat when the river rose. When he put the cabin up on the pilings, he had made certain it was five feet above the hundred-year high water mark. Even ten inches of rain would not flood the cabin.

As they ate the flounder and drank a good white wine, the forecasters changed their prediction. The hurricane would go inland before it swung to the north. But still it was predicted to pass to the east of their position.

Already it was raining, and the wind was loud in the trees.

"We could leave," she said.

"I thought you liked to ride out hurricanes," he said.

"I do. I just want to make sure you're comfortable."

"We're not going to end up in the bass boat if that's what you mean. It'd take Noah's flood for that to happen."

"Let's not think about the storm anymore."

He switched off the TV.

"I'm not thinking about the storm at all," he said. "Besides it's going to blow itself out over land."

They ate bread pudding he made for dessert and then started to drink another bottle of wine. The wind had picked up. From time to time they heard the sound of branches falling. The rain sounded like gravel being hurled against the roof. The lights flickered on and off. He lit the gas lanterns. Then the power was gone and they were left with the hard white light of the lanterns. He would not start the generator for four or five hours, to make his fuel supply last as long as possible. As long as they kept the door to the refrigerator closed, the food would be all right.

In spite of what he had said, he was thinking about the storm. He found himself calculating over and over again the rise in the river ten inches of rain might produce and how the land would receive the water. It should be as predictable as the rise of the Nile, the water harmlessly spreading out over the flat land.

He poured her another glass of wine and put his arm around her. She leaned her head against his shoulder.

"We'll wait for the storm," she said.

"It sounds to me like the storm's already here," he said.

"No, not yet. I want the river to rise."

A large branch hit the roof. They heard it slide toward the ground, but it stopped, hanging over the edge of the screen porch for a moment before it fell. He wondered what lovemaking would be like during the height of the storm. He imagined a section of the roof sailing off in the wind.

"You've always been a lover of storms?" he asked.

"Since I was a child," she said. "I'd lie in bed on one of those summer nights in the Delta when it was too hot to sleep and watch the lightning flash way off in the distance. You can see for miles and miles in the Delta. We had a house at the edge of town. From my window there were cotton and soybean and rice fields all the way to the river. And I'd wish that storm would move our way. Afterwards it was easy to sleep in that coolness."

The wind increased and more debris was thrown against the house. She got up and went to the window.

"I believe we are going to get a piece of Anne," she said. "Look, the river's come up already."

He joined her and looked out the window. The bass boat had floated off the trailer. It surprised him the river had come up so fast but he said nothing.

They stopped drinking wine and switched to bottled water. He had a slight headache; his mouth felt dry. He drank up a whole bottle of water and opened another one. He might even have fallen asleep on the couch beside her except for the violence of the storm. Once he wanted to start the generator, but she said that would interfere with her pleasure of listening to the sounds of the storm.

As he was telling her how his family's house had escaped burning by Sherman, it was suddenly quiet outside.

"The eye!" she said. "We're in the eye!"

They went out on the screened porch with flashlights. A section of screen had been ripped from the wall and the gum branch that did the job was lying on the cypress boards. He played his light over the water below, which had risen half way up the pilings. It was brown and covered with leaves and branches and moving slowly toward the sea.

***

They began to make love in the calm of the eye, something that surprised him, for he would have expected she'd want to wait for the second half of the storm. But then he realized she was anticipating the return of the wind and rain. He could feel her about to come when she put her hand flat against his chest and pushed him away. They lay together on their backs. Through the skylight they could see the stars. The skylight had a history of leaking. He had resealed it at the beginning of the summer.

"We'll wait for the storm," she said.

He thought all this was ridiculous, that anyone would laugh at what he had already done to get her into bed, but at this point he found it impossible to do anything but accede to her wishes.

During the time the time it took the eye to pass over them, he lay on his back looking up at The Whale, his favorite constellation of late summer. She was asleep. But when the rain and wind began again, she woke and they made love again. Then gradually the force of the wind began to abate. Before he drifted off to sleep he looked up at the skylight, a lighter rectangle against the darkness, and wondered when it was going to start to leak.

***

When he woke, light was coming through the skylight. The rain and wind had stopped. There was the sound of water moving against the pilings. She was sleeping soundly beside him.

His first thought was that he had neglected to start the generator. He got up and went into the living room on his way to the kitchen. There he was stopped by the strangeness of the view. He picked his camera up off the table and began to take pictures. The water was almost level with the cypress boards on which he was standing. He had no idea how fast the river was rising, but it surely would continue for at least another day as its flooded tributaries fed water into it. He checked on the bass boat. Its cover was intact so he would not have to bail it out.

He woke her and they dressed. They found a large rattlesnake coiled on the top step. He lifted the rattlesnake off the step with a fishing pole. The snake offered no resistance but gracefully swam over to pile of logs and trash caught between two trees. He carefully removed the cover and was relieved no snakes had managed to crawl under it.

By the time they had taken seats in the boat the water had risen over the step where the rattlesnake had taken refuge.

"I never would have believed the water could come up so quickly," she said.

"It won't wash the cabin away," he said. "But I'll have to clean the turtles and cottonmouths out of the bedroom."

He used the trolling motor to maneuver the bass boat through the trees and out into the cornfield. His plan was to cross the slough and reach the private levee on the other side. The water was littered with dead animals: cows, pigs, chickens, turkeys. There were plastic containers of all sorts and colors. A yellow whale, some child's beach toy, floated next to a dead hog. A helicopter passed overhead but did not linger. He shot up most of his remaining film.

They reached the edge of the slough and he took the boat through an opening in the trees. A strong current in the slough caught the boat and overwhelmed the power of the trolling motor, sweeping them downstream, the opposite direction he wished to go. He started the engine and brought the boat under control. He looked for the twin chimneys that marked the house until he saw one through the trees. At the next opening he took the boat out of the current and through the treeline.

He heard the sound of fast-moving water. He maneuvered the boat through a screen of small trees and as they came out into the open where a soybean field lay beneath them, he saw that the house was gone, a lone chimney remaining. The levee had broken.

"Oh, Constantine, it's all washed away," she said.

"Lucky for Mr. Troy the summers are too hot to suit him," he said. "My aunt will be happy."

"What?"

"Some of my family would rather nobody have it if they can't."

He told her how one of his aunts had written him a formal note in her spidery old woman's handwriting to tell him she wished the house had been burned by Sherman rather than fall into the hands of people from New Hampshire.

He steered the boat through the break in the levee and into the dead water behind the remaining chimney. The dining room table he had sold to the banker was floating about, providing refuge to two white turkeys, the sort raised by the hundreds in long narrow sheds. They were too fat to fly. But these had learned how to swim and had somehow reached the table before being drowned by the weight of their wet feathers.

He imagined she was thinking of the fate of her machinery and he tried to form a picture in his mind of how far the nearest slough or creek was to her storage building and how high the ground was. He had never done a survey on that land.

"Your equipment?" he asked.

"I don't know," she said. "It's insured."

He put his arm around her.

"Maybe you weren't flooded at all," he said.

"I hope not."

80

"You too. There's your office."

"No, it's on high ground. I'm all right there."

He wondered if he were falling in love with this woman or if his feelings were caused by the strangeness of their experience together.

"Are you still going to be traveling to hurricanes?" he asked.

"Maybe not," she said. "But that eye was wonderful, wasn't it."

"What would we be like together without a hurricane?"

"I'm satisfied with hurricanes."

"Me too."

He was reluctant to speak of love. He looked out over the flooded land. Soon the dead would begin to swell and stink. Somewhere, he supposed, there were people too.

"Snakes and dead hogs," she said.

"Yes, and turkeys that learned to swim," he said.

He pointed the camera at her.

"Just make sure there's nothing dead in it," she said.

He did, composing the picture so that the line of cypresses that marked the slough was in the background. Then she took a picture of him. After that he set the camera on an ice chest and programmed it take a picture of both of them. He put his arms around her and the shutter clicked.

"After The Great Flood," she said. "Will that do as a title?"

"I think so," he said.

Off in the distance, beyond a line of trees, the metal roofs of Mr. Atkins' chicken houses gleamed in the sun. He had done the survey for the land when Mr. Atkins bought it. He remembered the elevation, a fact that did not surprise him, for his memory for such details was perfect. It was three times the elevation of the site of his family house. They could take refuge there.

Pure Water

THE reconnaissance patrol came out of the trees into the park-like space that held the Montagnard village. They had been away from their base camp for ten days. It was the dry season and the red clay, beaten to a fine dust by the passage of the village's herd of ponies, rose in little puffs from beneath their boots. There were five of them. They were minus one man, a Montagnard scout called Bear, who had died after being bitten by a poisonous snake.

This was not Bear's village. Rembert Williams, who carried the radio, was not sure exactly where his village was. But they would know everything at II Corps headquarters in Pleiku. Bear's real name, whatever unpronounceable collection of syllables that was, and the name of the village where he was born was in some file along with how much he had been paid each month to scout for the Americans.

The night before he died Bear had slept with his arms around Rembert. Lukasavage, who slept that night on the other side of Rembert, smelled of the butterscotch candy his aunt sent him from home. Sergeant Hansen was always complaining that the smell was going to give away their position. It was cold on the mountains at night and they huddled together to stay warm. At first light Bear had gotten up to relieve Fielding, who was standing watch, leaving Rembert to shiver under his poncho.

Bear had stepped on the snake. He had given a little cry when it had bitten him, a cry that awoke the entire patrol. Sergeant Hansen killed the snake with the butt of his rifle. It had been easy to kill, rendered sluggish by the cold. The snake would probably have slipped away at Bear's approach if it could have moved fast enough.

They all stood in a circle around Bear while Fielding knelt over him. He said something to Fielding, who had learned to speak some of Bear's Montagnard dialect, but afterwards Fielding said he could not understand what Bear had said. They buried him on the mountain and camouflaged the grave. Sergeant Hansen wrote down the coordinates so that after the war the people from his village could give him a proper burial in accordance with their religion. No one had any idea what sort of snake it was, only that it was not a cobra.

"It don't matter," Fielding said. "It's the kind of snake that when it bites you, you sit down and die."

Half a mile from the village the Montagnards had tapped a spring by driving bamboo pipes into a hillside. The water gushed out of three pipes and fell into a pool below. That was where Sergeant Hansen was leading the patrol. Their canteens were empty. It had been a long hot walk down the side of the mountain. They had drunk from the Montagnard spring before.

Sergeant Hansen, a Tennessean, was now doing his third tour in Vietnam. Lukasavage was from Cleveland, Dexter from Texas, and Fielding from Los Angeles. Rembert, the son of a Mississippi farmer, was the only one who had been to college, the only one who was married. When asked what a college boy like him was doing in Vietnam and he told them he had volunteered, his questioners always laughed in disbelief.

"That water is gonna be so good," Dexter said.

He was the son of a fundamentalist minister.

"We'll baptize you again," Lukasavage said. "Just like your old man does to people in Texas."

Dexter grinned. "Sure, you go right ahead. I've been saved. Won't no Catholic baptism harm me."

"I just want a cold beer," Fielding said.

"And a hot shower," Rembert said.

They had located the North Vietnamese base camp they were searching for and had monitored troop movements. Later from a ridge top they watched a B-52 strike on the narrow valley that held the base camp. But Rembert had no faith in B-52 strikes. The North Vietnamese were hidden deep in tunnels, beyond the reach of the bombs.

"No gold again, Rembert," Sergeant Hansen said. "Every time I go out with you I think I'm gonna come home rich."

They knew Rembert was interested in locating temples hidden in the forest. They thought he was after gold or jewels. Rembert let them think so. It was art that he was after. Rembert's hero, André Malraux, had tried that over in Cambodia. He and his wife had barely escaped prison, but he had ended up as minister of culture in France. Malraux had gone on to do great things. He had discovered the site in Arabia of the Queen of Sheba's city. With the money he made from the sale of the art, Rembert planned on financing expeditions.

Rembert had resolved he would be more careful in Southeast Asia than Malraux had been. He would find sites no one knew about. As soon as he had completed his tour he would come back. The South Vietnamese were totally corrupt and could be bribed. But despite the inquiries he had made among the Montagnards he had not located a single temple.

"I guess I'm going home poor," Rembert said.

They all laughed.

At the spring they came upon a woman bathing her child, a male infant only six or seven months old. She stood knee-deep in the pool, bent at the waist, with the baby resting on her back. She balanced him there while she used her hands to wash herself. The boy wore a single brass ring around his ankle. As they approached she turned her back to them but continued splashing water on herself.

Rembert was struck by the scene. It was like something from Gauguin. As they came closer he noticed piles of water buffalo dung scattered about. Everywhere there were flies, so many their communal buzz competed with the rush of the water.

They all dropped their rucksacks and lit cigarettes. Rembert tried not to stare at the woman but the others, except for Dexter, were watching her intently. Dexter had become suddenly interested in making sure the rounds were seated properly in the magazine of his rifle.

She came out of the pool and wound a piece of black silk about herself and another one about the child. She tied a woven sash, made of brightly dyed yarns, around her waist and pulled her long straight black hair back with a thong.

Fielding went over and began talking with her in pidgin English and a few words of Montagnard. The rest, Rembert with them, waded into the pool, their rifles slung over their shoulders, and drank directly from the water coming out of the pipes. Then they filled their canteens.

They sat on the grass next to the pool and drank the cold water. At the top of the slight rise behind them was a huge banyan tree. The hillside above the pool was covered with a stand of bamboo.

"Best water in Vietnam," Dexter said. "Even that stuff we drink in base camp has got Agent Orange in it. And chlorine. It's not natural."

"I didn't know you were a hippie," Lukasavage said.

Dexter ignored him.

"There're some springs near my house," Dexter said. "But the water tastes of sulfur."

Fielding came over to them. The woman was sitting on the grass a little distance away, nursing the child. She had her head bent over the child, watching the boy suck on her nipple. She seemed pleased at his eager hunger.

"She says she'll do it," Fielding said. "She wants cigarettes and money."

Rembert looked at the woman, who now had her head up, her gaze fixed on the top of the banyan tree.

"Like the Madonna," Fielding said.

"Shut your mouth," Lukasavage said.

"I forget," Fielding said. "You're killing gooks for Christ."

Lukasavage did not bother to reply.

Fielding started to say something else but Sergeant Hansen cut him off.

"That's enough, Fielding," Sergeant Hansen said.

They collected money and cigarettes, piling them up on the grass beside the pool. Then they played the paper, scissors, rock game to decide who would go first.

Rembert did not contribute or play the game. The others ignored him. He sat crosslegged on the grass with his rifle across his legs. He took out his wife Cassie's latest letter and read it. It was spring in Mississippi. The dogwoods and azaleas were in bloom. The ancient pink dogwood in the front yard of her house had not bloomed, stricken by some unknown blight. Now it had been cut down and she had planted a new one. She wrote that next spring they would watch the new tree bloom together.

A shadow fell over him. He looked up and saw the woman before him. She smiled at him. He stood up. She held out the child

86

to him.

"A babysitter," Fielding said.

He ignored Fielding and took the child in his arms. The weight of the child, heavier than he had imagined, surprised him. The child was warm, so warm he suspected the boy might have a fever. Then the remembrance of the warmth of Bear's body came into his mind, overlaid with the smell of butterscotch.

Dexter went first. He and the woman strolled around the pool and into the stand of bamboo. The patrol lolled about on the grass and smoked.

Rembert thought of his mother sitting in a rocking chair on the screened porch with him in her arms. She had done a drawing of them which Rembert kept in his bedroom.

His mother had been dead for years. His father met her in Romania while he was working for the OSS during World War II. She was a Romanian Jew who had left art school to join a partisan group. She came to Mississippi with his father, to the house in the Mississippi Delta just below Memphis, but she soon felt stifled by life on the farm. His father built her a studio behind the house, next to the farm shop. He encouraged her to work in cypress, a wood she found exotic. She shaped it into stylized figures connected with the Delta landscape: rattlesnakes, deer, turtles, alligators.

She went to live in Paris after she and his father had divorced. He was preparing to go to Paris to spend the summer with her when she was killed in a car accident.

Rembert and his father had argued over his joining the army after his freshman year at Harvard.

"You're a damned fool," his father said.

"You parachuted into Romania," Rembert said. "Lots of folks might have said the same about you."

"This war in Vietnam is hopeless. I don't want you to get yourself killed for nothing."

But finally his father said that he understood, promised Rembert he would look after Cassie while he was gone.

"I didn't expect to live when I jumped out of that plane," he said. "I'd stopped worrying about living at all. I just concentrated on the mission. I want you to think about living, count on it."

Rembert promised he would concentrate on living. Cassie was convinced he would return from the war. He told her the usual things soldiers tell the people they leave behind at home, that he would take care of himself, that he would be lucky. But her confidence in his safety went beyond reason. It was as if she had received a promise from some god that he would be protected. He hoped she would not fall apart if he were killed. His father would understand. She would not. Cassie knew about his plan to locate art for future theft. But he never said a word to his father about his plan to emulate the life of Malraux.

***

Dexter returned and Lukasavage strolled off into the bamboo. Dexter went off a few yards away and sat down in the shade next to the pool, his back to them. A breeze stirred the tops of the bamboo that grew over the pool, causing patterns of light and shadow to play across the water. Everyone was embarrassed.

It had not been at all like this when just before they had gone out on this patrol they had all visited a brothel in Pleiku. There was a bar set up on the roof of a house with a view of the town and the mountains over into Laos. But the view was spoiled by the razor wire strung on rusted metal poles along the edge of the rooftop.

They all were dressed in silk bathrobes and wore shoulder holsters. Girls hung on their arms. They strutted and smiled big smiles and took their pistols in and out of their holsters for the girls to admire. He liked how the weight of the pistol felt under his robe.

When it grew dark, they went down to the rooms below. Just as they left the roof, a fire base on a ridgetop began to take rocket and mortar fire. The firebase's artillery replied. A gunship went up and its gatling gun sent down an unbroken stream of red tracers.

"They're probing," Fielding said.

"Could be a heavy dew tonight," Dexter said. "I'm sure glad it ain't gonna fall on us."

Rembert had put his arm around the girl beside him. She was drunk. He wished she had not gotten so drunk. One thing he had learned about himself was that he felt no guilt over being unfaithful to Cassie. The girl meant nothing to him. Tomorrow he might die in an ambush. He knew this was the usual soldier logic and the banality of it, the fact that he was doing what a thousand other soldiers were doing, slightly disturbed him. Then he wished he were drunk too, just as drunk as the girl.

The child whimpered. He rocked it in his arms; the child closed his eyes and slept. Sergeant Hansen and Fielding were stretched out on the grass. Fielding had pulled his bush hat over his face to keep the flies way. Hansen ignored them. Dexter was floating on his back in the pool. He had piled his clothes next to the water and set his rifle on top of them.

Lukasavage appeared and sat down beside Fielding, who got up and walked off into the bamboo. Rembert brushed flies away from the child's face. He felt sleepy. He thought of spending his coming leave with Cassie in Hawaii. He would sleep, eat, make love and for a week not think of the war at all. But if he had been forced to choose one of those three things, it would have been sleep.

The baby awoke and began to whimper again. Lukasavage walked over to Rembert and took one of the child's hands between his fingers. The child wrapped his hand around Lukasavage's index finger. Lukasavage put his free hand on the baby's forehead.

"He's got a fever," Lukasavage said.

"Babies feel hot," Rembert said.

Rembert could remember one of his aunts saying that.

"He could have malaria," Lukasavage said.

"No, he'd be burning up if he had that," Rembert said.

He looked over at Sergeant Hansen and wondered how someone could ever learn to sleep with his face covered with flies.

"He don't have a cold," Lukasavage said.

Rembert could feel the sweaty place made against his fatigue jacket by the heat of the baby. He considered all the diseases the child might have: typhus, cholera, bubonic plague. Or he might have something that did not even have a name, some unnamed virus sprung up out of the rain forest.

Lukasavage lay down and closed his eyes.

Fielding returned and woke Sergeant Hansen. Then Fielding stood at the edge of the pool and said something to Dexter who was still floating about on his back. Fielding walked over to Dexter's rucksack and opened it. He took out something wrapped in plastic from which he produced two cigars. He lit one and gave it to Dexter. He lit the other for himself. For a time Dexter stood waist deep in the pool and smoked. Then he managed to float on his back and smoke. Fielding applauded. Lukasavage woke up and went over to Dexter's rucksack and helped himself to a cigar.

"That's my last one," Dexter said.

"I'll buy you a whole box at the PX," Lukasavage said.

Rembert lay down and closed his eyes while the child lay sleeping against his chest. The child burped; he smelled the sour scent of the woman's milk. He tried adopting Sergeant Hansen's method and let the flies land on his face, but he could not manage that. He wished he had a piece of mosquito netting to put over his face. Instead he did like Dexter and hid his face under his bush hat. It smelled of dirt and his own sweat, but at least the flies could not get at him.

He slept and dreamed that he was parachuting out of a plane at night. He jumped toward a single light at low altitude. He pulled the rip cord immediately. But the parachute did not open and he was falling and falling. He awoke to someone shaking him. He looked up into the face of Sergeant Hansen.

"She's waiting," Sergeant Hansen said. "It's free. For looking after the baby."

He sat up. The child did not awaken.

"I've got to take care of this baby," he said.

"I'll take care of him," Sergeant Hansen said.

Sergeant Hansen picked up the child. The child woke and gave a little cry. Then he settled back against Hansen's chest.

"I know about babies," Sergeant Hansen said.

He looked at Fielding and Lukasavage who were all smoking cigars and talking to Dexter who still stood in the pool.

"You go on," Sergeant Hansen said.

Rembert picked up his rifle and started across the grass.

"You won't need that," Fielding said.

They all laughed but Rembert ignored them. And then Rembert, who up until this point had no particular desire for the woman and had intended to go tell her it was all over, that she had fulfilled her part of the bargain and could return to her child, felt himself overwhelmed with desire.

He found the woman lying in a sort of alcove in the bamboo. He had lain in ambushes in such places. The accumulation of leaves made a soft bed, a good place to sleep. The bamboo stalks, many as thick as his leg, arched overhead like the flying buttresses of some green cathedral. She had wrapped herself up again in the length of black silk. She smiled at him, a beatific serene sort of smile, not at all the smile of a woman who had serviced four soldiers and was preparing for a fifth.

When he knelt down beside her and placed his hand on her

breast, he heard the sound of the first mortar round being dropped, followed by four others.

"Incoming!" Sergeant Hansen yelled.

The woman tried to get up but he pulled her down. She screamed something in her dialect as the first round hit. Pieces of bamboo, lopped off by the shell fragments, fell on top of the them, followed by a shower of water thrown up by a direct hit on the pool. Then he was up and running, the woman close behind him.

They came out of the bamboo. He saw the bodies strewn about and knew they were all dead, the child too. It had been a marvelous bit of shooting on the part of the North Vietnamese gunners. He grabbed the radio, luckily still intact, and a cloth bandolier of magazines. The woman was screaming over the child. As he ran away from the pool, he heard the sound of other rounds being dropped and then a few seconds later the impacts.

He ran through the scrub in the direction of the base camp. Someone with a view of the pool was directing the fire. They would now be hunting him. He hid himself in a clump of bamboo and called for a helicopter on the radio. He told them he was between the village and the base camp.

The pilot instructed him to stay put.

"No," he said. "I'm running. You watch for me in the scrub."

He ran through the scrub, hoping to put some distance between himself and his pursuers. Then he heard the sound of the helicopter. He called the pilot on the radio and stepped out into an open space. The helicopter appeared above him and immediately began taking fire, which the door gunner returned. A Cobra gunship appeared, made a rocket run, and the fire ceased. The pilot put the helicopter down in the scrub, kicking up a cloud of red dust.

The helicopter took off before he was well inside, the gunner wrapping his arms around his chest and pulling him backwards so that they both lay sprawled on the floor for a moment. The helicopter rose quickly and turned over the scrub, and he could see the pool for a moment and the smoke and dust from the impact of the rockets and then a piece of the river that came out of the gorge that held the North Vietnamese base camp.

The gunner ran his hands over him and yelled in his ear, asking him if he was all right and he nodded his head, but he knew that he was not all right. It was not the death of his friends, although that was part of it. He tried to imagine how he would now feel if he had spent his time with the woman and there had been no mortar attack and at this moment the woman was walking back to the village with the child in her arms and he was walking through the scrub with the patrol. But he could not imagine that. So he tried to think of nothing at all as the helicopter began to make its descent into the base camp.

84 Avenue Foch

WHEN my father was a boy in Paris, he took pictures of Gestapo Headquarters. Or at least he claimed he did. I've never seen a single photograph. When he and his father fled Pairs, the photographs were left behind. His explanation was that people on the run could not afford to be caught with such incriminating evidence. Even for a man given to extravagant tales (if he shot two ducks he would say it was twenty and some of them would be a rare and seldom seen species on top of that), his Paris stories always seemed to me, at least once I had left behind the naïve credulity of my childhood years, outrageous.

My grandfather Jean-Henri, a French petroleum engineer, the son of an American woman from New Orleans and a French chemist, was working for British intelligence. Several years before the outbreak of the war my grandfather was involved with the construction of a refinery in Romania. There he met and fell in love with my grandmother. They married and he brought her home to live in Paris. After the fall of France, they joined the underground.

The Nazis in my father's tales were not TV or movie Nazis, easily tricked to satisfy the requirements of a plot. He was fooling around with the counter-intelligence branch of the Gestapo. I just could not believe they'd allow anyone to take photographs of the building. My father claimed that he told the Germans he was playing hooky from school. Supposedly the guards admired that. There was a good explanation for why my father was allowed to run about the streets. His mother was not there. Someone betrayed Ylenia to the Germans while she was on a mission in Lyon. She was executed at Natzweiler.

The camera belonged to Ylenia, who studied painting in Romania. Sometime I've wondered if she'd have become a better photographer than my father. He did end up becoming a photographer, although a part-time one. And he did take some terrific pictures.

So what would have happened if SS Sturmbannführer Josef Kieffer glanced out the window from his office on the fourth floor and there was my father taking pictures with his mother's camera? If I'd asked my father that question, he'd probably have said, unable to resist embellishing a good story, that Sturmbannführer Kieffer came down and posed for him, perhaps even snapped a photo of my father saluting one of the guards. Or maybe he let him take a photo of a prisoner being carried off to Fresnes prison after an interrogation.

My father had plenty of true stories to tell. But he refused to talk about his father's work as a British agent. And no matter how many times I asked, he would not tell me about their escape over the Pyrenees. After Jean-Henri learned of Ylenia's capture, he realized he had to leave Paris. Ylenia might reveal everything under torture. There was absolutely nothing he could do for her. And he had my father to consider. As it turned out Ylenia told the Nazis nothing. I wonder if my father ever told Jean-Henri that right up to the day they left he was wandering about on Avenue Foch with a camera.

They made their way to Perpingnan and walked over the Pyrenees. They sailed to America where Jean-Henri's mother, who had long ago divorced his father, had returned to New Orleans and remarried. My grandfather died before the war was over, leaving my father to be raised by his mother, who died just after my father graduated from MIT. So I never heard my grandfather's version of those days in Paris. But my father was happy to talk about photographing 84 Avenue Foch any time I asked. Then as I grew older I stopped asking. I suppose my father's fantasy may have been a way of avoiding talking about things he preferred not to recall.

I'm in Paris from time to time. You'd think I'd go by 84 Avenue Foch. But I've not been a single time. To visit that place would be to buy into my father's fabrication. And even if what he told me was true, even a small part of it, the trail has long ago grown cold.

***

My father died recently. On the way to a cabin we own on Lake Ponchatrain, he fell out of the pirogue he was poling through the marsh and drowned. I recall when he built the pirogue himself, using an adz to hew it out of a big cypress log. He was that sort of man. The day it happened was clear and calm. The autopsy revealed nothing other than water in his lungs, no heart attack as everyone suspected. My grandmother and grandfather had died of heart attacks. Bad hearts on both sides of the family. I suppose I should watch my diet and exercise more, but I don't. Two weeks after my father's death, my mother had a stroke. She's able to talk, but there are times when she makes no sense at all. I go and see her almost every day.

I own a fence and wall company. Lots of people in New Orleans are interested in putting fences and walls around things these days. We'll even top a wall with broken grass from wine bottles. It's expensive because of labor costs, but lots of folks are willing to pay. They think it looks better than razor wire. I've never married, just a succession of girl friends. For the last three years it's been a woman named Alice, who's a federal hydrologist. Her job is to help make sure the Mississippi River keeps running past New Orleans and doesn't jump into the Atchafalaya River, turning the current river into an estuary of the Gulf. The River Control Structure, the Corps of Engineers' fancy name for a dam, is the only thing that's keeping it from doing that. Alice says that one of these springs when the river rises it's going to happen. I think her job makes her look at life in a pessimistic manner that's not good for her.

We're thinking about getting married. Neither of us wants children. We go to Saints' games; we shoot ducks; we eat at fine restaurants. We have a good time. She grew up in Covington just across Lake Ponchatrain. I feel comfortable with her. Ten years ago, I was thinking about going back to graduate school (I have a degree in philosophy from Tulane), but now I know that's not going to happen.

My father became a petroleum engineer just like his father. But his passion was photography. We always spent our summer vacations living in a tent in the North Carolina mountains. We went up those remote creeks, sometimes on horseback, and there, surrounded by that luxuriant vegetation (rhododendrons, mountain laurel, gum, ash, and hemlock), the rush of the creek singing in our ears, he'd take pictures of my mother. Mostly nude. I can recall that I never thought it was strange, his doing that. When I turned eleven, they sent me off to a summer camp in those same mountains. I never went with them again, but I saw the new photographs, the results of those trips.

He always posed my mother in claustrophobic places: undercut banks, narrow passages between boulders, rhododendron thickets. Sometimes there would just be a piece of her showing: a leg, a single breast, a hand. Never her face. Now I wish that they'd taken me with them.

"Did he take pictures of Gestapo headquarters?" I ask my mother.

"Surely he did," she said. "He was there."

The nursing home is an excellent one. My father was frugal and saved his money. My mother will never have to touch the principal on his investments.

"Did you ever see a picture?" I ask.

"Oh, he took lots of pictures," she says.

He hung the mountain pictures about the house, but by the time I was old enough to notice how people might react, all their friends were used to them. And by that time the young woman in those pictures didn't seem like my mother at all. I wonder if the main attraction of the 84 Avenue Foch pictures for me is that they don't exist. Those pictures of my mother are real, but sometimes don't seem real to me.

"They went over the mountains," she said.

There are no pictures of the Pyrenees either. The trip over the Pyrenees was real and there are no pictures. The excursions to 84 Avenue Foch are not real and there are no pictures. Maybe my father forgot to take the camera. Or left it because they were traveling light. Moving fast through the mountains under the cover of darkness.

***

My mother is allowed to go home, to the house she and my father built in Metairie. She no longer slides off into incoherency. But her left arm is still mostly paralyzed. Now I wish I were not the only child. If I had a sister, she would take over the job of caring for my mother. That's still expected. My mother has hired a night and day nurse. She seems to enjoy having them there. One is a white woman and the other black. My mother jokes with them as they watch TV together and play cards. Sometimes I play too, although I take no pleasure from games like that.

My mother and I are playing hearts one afternoon. I've dropped by after I've checked on a nearby project. One of my crews is putting broken glass in the top of a wall. When I walked up, they were smashing wine bottles. I imagined the finished project: the sun shining on the glass and green lizards, who've adjusted their skin color to match that of the glass, slipping in and out between the shards set in cement atop the wall.

"You're not paying attention," my mother says.

"You know I'm not much for card games," I say.

"Just like your father."

"He played."

"With just as about the enthusiasm as you."

I drift off again and play badly and pretty soon the game is over. Samantha, the day nurse, comes in and tells her that one of her favorite soaps is about to come on. It's one of Samantha's favorites too. Samantha was a star basketball player in high school. I remember reading about her in the paper. She had a scholarship to LSU but then something happened. I can't recall if it was an injury or something else. But she never played. Once I drove into the driveway just after her shift had changed and found her shooting three pointers at my old goal. We played a couple of one on one games. I didn't have a chance.

Samantha goes off to make coffee. They'll drink coffee and eat stale beignets left over from breakfast. My mother is supposed to stop eating things like that, but she's never paid any attention to doctors.

I get up to leave.

"Those pictures you were asking about," my mother says.

It amazes me that she remembers our conversation.

"He left them in Paris," I say. "I understand why. They couldn't afford to get caught with them."

"No, he brought them with him."

I think this is all the aftermath of the stroke. I try to imagine the state of her mind, a tangle of memories and dreams. It must be impossible for her sometimes to sort out what's real.

"He put them somewhere. I just can't remember where. His camera things are up in the attic. Maybe the pictures are in with them. I can't really remember."

"Mrs. Foix, it's about to start," Samantha calls.

I tell myself not to buy into this, but I do start thinking about the attic.

Then Samantha appears and my mother takes her arm. They disappear into the TV room. I resolve to not allow myself to start searching the house for something that's not there.

***

It's my birthday, and Alice and I have lunch at Antione's to celebrate. She knows all about the pictures by now. She's sensible and advises me not to start looking. She can't understand why I'm so obsessed with those pictures. That's the word she uses, "obsessed."

After lunch she gives me a present. It's in a small square box with a weight to it that makes me think what's inside is small but dense. I wonder if it is a pair of field glasses. We were down at the cabin the week before to look at the birds. It's September so there aren't any ducks yet but plenty of other birds. I dropped my field glasses over the side of the pirogue, and I haven't gotten around to replacing them.

But when I unwrap the paper I discover that it's a camera, an old Leica, the kind my father used.

"Like Cartier-Bresson," Alice says. "Minimalist equipment."

She tells me that she bought it at a photography shop specializing in old cameras. It's been reconditioned and is in perfect working order. I suppose I could go up into the attic and dig my father's camera out of an old trunk. But I realize that I prefer to have my own."

"Take pictures," she says. "Don't look for them."

Over the next few weeks my mother makes rapid improvement. She even gains a little use of her arm. I practice with the camera. It seems strange to me that I never was interested in taking pictures. I watched my father do it and that seemed to satisfy me. But I take no pictures of people. Instead I take pictures of walls and fences. When I get the film developed, even I can see that I don't have much talent.

One Saturday Alice and I make dinner for my mother. We use an old Creole recipe for duck, *canard aux navets*. Then we have dinner around the big table in the dining room. Through the windows I see the open sweep of the lawn to the street. I put a fence around the back yard. I'd like to do the same for the front, maybe a tall iron fence with a remote controlled gate, but I know my mother would never consent to such a project.

After dinner we talk for a while and then my mother goes off to bed. Alice switches from wine to a good cognac my father favored. Pretty soon I bring up the subject of the Avenue Foch pictures.

"You're just not going to leave it alone," Alice says.

"I think they're somewhere in this house," I say.

"Have you looked?"

"Not yet. I've just been thinking about where they might be."

Then I'm surprised when she suggests we go look in the attic. We carry the bottle of cognac with us. We meet Samantha in the hall. She's switched shifts with Louise this week. Something about Louise's mother. She tells us that my mother is already sound asleep. Samantha has a book in her hand, Adolph Rupp's book on how to coach basketball. She tells us that she's thinking about coaching. She plans on going back to school and getting her teaching certificate.

"Yawl just let me know when you leave," she says. "I want to make sure the door's locked."

I'm bad about leaving it unlocked. She's scolded me for that. I know she carries a Glock in her purse. She's taking no chances in a dangerous city. I like knowing that she won't have to depend on the police. Sometimes in New Orleans when you call the police and they show up, pretty soon you start wishing that you'd taken your chances with the criminals.

Alice seems to have some sort of method, because she starts right in on one of the trunks that are stacked against the wall. That one turns out to be full of those metallic, silvery finished Christmas ornaments from the 40s and 50s. The second is packed with my mother's college textbooks and notebooks. A third is filled with my father's photographic equipment, but there are no pictures. Then while I'm lifting a Persian rug off two trunks, Alice gives a cry of delight. When I turn around, she's holding up a plate. She's kneeling beside a huge trunk.

"The Sevres china," she says.

Then I realize that she doesn't think the pictures exist at all, that she knew the china was there all the time.

We take out the plates wrapped in pages from *The Times Picuyne.*

"It's a complete service for twelve," she says. "A wedding present from your cousin in Paris. It's never been used. Your mother unpacked it and then put it away. She didn't tell me why."

It seems to me that Alice and my mother have marriage on their minds.

"She asked me to look," Alice says. "She wants to start using it."

I think of my mother giving dinner parties for twelve. I remember when she and my father used to do that.

We carry the beautiful china down the stairs and stack it on the dining room table.

"Let's go open trunks," Alice suggests.

"More china?" I ask.

"No, those photographs."

So we go back up into the attic and go through all of the trunks. We find the tent, sleeping bags, and mosquito bars from those trips to North Carolina. But we don't find a single photograph of any sort.

We sit on an old daybed that once was in my father's office and drink more of the cognac. Then we make love. I realize that china and lovemaking were what Alice had on her mind all along. We lie on our backs on the daybed for a long time and talk. I think of my father sleeping on the daybed in his office as he was accustomed to do. The mattress is bare now. No hint of the scent of his pipe. The smell I do notice is that of cypress, much stronger in this corner of the attic. I noticed the smell when Alice and I were making love. Then I see the holes in the ceiling made by carpenter bees and the little piles of cypress dust that have sifted to the floor. I suspect there's a broken pane in the window at this end of the attic.

"Would you like to live in this house when Mother dies?" I ask.

"She has beautiful things," Alice says.

I don't quite know what to make of that answer. Alice wanted the china, but *that* had never been used.

"You can buy new things," I say.

Alice looks around the attic. I wonder if she is imagining those photographs of my mother packed away in some trunk. Or the dining room table disassembled and stored in one corner, the legs and extra leaves stacked on the top.

"Yes, I could do that," Alice says. "But you'll have to give up the idea of finding photographs of that Gestapo building in this house."

"I'll stop," I say.

I intend to stop. I have no intention of opening all the trunks again and looking for false bottoms, secret compartments that open with the push of a button.

"Good," she says. "*That* will make me happy."

We get dressed and go downstairs. We find Samantha sitting at the kitchen table reading her Adolph Rupp book. She's got one of those portable boards that basketball coaches use in games and she's diagramming plays with a dry erase pencil.

"The man was a genius," she says.

I say, I don't know. I've never read the book, but I recall that he got results at Kentucky.

"Mrs. Foix is sound sleep," she says. "Don't forget to lock that door. I don't want ruffians in this house in the middle of the night."

I promise I will and we go out of the house. Alice makes me check the door twice. Then I drive her home.

***

Not long after Christmas I visit Alice out at the River Control Structure. She's promised me a ride in an army bridge boat. Periodically it's necessary to take samples from the bottom just behind the dam, because there's always the danger of the structure being undermined. My mother has made a complete recovery. Alice and I are planning to get married in May.

We go out in the boat; everyone wears big life preservers. Alice doesn't actually do the sampling, but she's in charge of supervising it. We watch two workers lower the sampling device, attached to a boom on the bow of the boat. The water boils beneath us, and the boat shudders. Alice gives orders to the men operating the cable and talks to the captain of the boat on a walkie-talkie. As he edges the boat up closer to the face of the dam, the men yell out readings to her. She writes the figures down in a notebook.

I take pictures of the work with the Leica. I've gotten better with it. I took a photography course at the University of New Orleans and learned a few things along with how to develop film.

Afterwards we go to a local restaurant for lunch. We order soft shell crabs.

"Well, is it going to survive the spring floods?" I ask.

She shrugs. "Who knows? Right now it looks all right. No big pockets."

Then I start telling her a story of a history professor I once had at Georgetown. I took some classes there one summer. I'm not surprised that I can't remember his name. He was a Cuban who had to leave when Fidel took over. The man went to school with Fidel. He showed us a class picture in which he was standing behind the young boy who would grow up and cause the United States so much trouble.

The professor spoke of wishing that he had a hammer in his hand. He made a downward stroke with the imaginary hammer. We all laughed at the thought of him smashing Fidel's skull.

"That has a connection with the river?" she asks.

"No, I was thinking of the Avenue Foch pictures. My father may have taken a photograph of an important prisoner. You know, he could have taken pictures of his own mother. They might have brought her to Paris."

"That's crazy. You told me she was captured in Lyon."

"That's true."

I try to remember how I got that information out of my father, but I can't remember. There's a possibility I read it in a book."

"I'll bet the CIA was picking that Cuban's brain about Fidel," she says.

"Probably," I say.

Then our crabs come and our attention turns to our food. After we eat we end up talking about plans for our wedding. Alice has never been married. She wants a traditional gown, a church wedding.

My mother dies in April. The cleaning women find her dead in the shower. There's no autopsy, but her doctor guesses that her heart gave out. After the funeral, I put my condo up for sale and move into the house. Alice starts spending the night there and pretty soon she's practically moved in too. But neither one of us is sure that we want to live there after we're married.

One day I come home and discover that Alice has put all the photographs of my mother in the attic.

"You don't mind?" she says.

"What about them bothers you?" I ask.

"I'm not sure. But you don't mind?"

"I don't think so."

I question Alice further about why the photographs make her uncomfortable. I discover that whatever it is, she can't articulate it. But it's clear that she likes the house better with the photographs in the attic. Right away I find myself missing them, but I don't say anything.

We have the church wedding Alice wanted. Alice puts her condo up for sale and moves all of her things into the house. From time to time I go up into the attic and sit on the daybed and look at my father's photographs. I no longer find myself wondering if I'll come upon those pictures of Avenue Foch in the house. There was a moment when I opened the safe deposit at the bank that I thought my father might have kept them there, but it was full of the usual things: titles to the cars, the deed to the house, some bonds to swamp land that I expect are more or less worthless unless someone suddenly finds oil there. So far all the land has produced is a few dry holes.

We settle into living in the house, and I'm happy. I think that this is what my father and mother must have felt like when they first began their life there. I wonder if he were already taking pictures of my mother then or if that happened afterwards. His career was on a upward trajectory at the oil company. I imagine that they were both thinking they would have a good life in the house. I suppose that's exactly what happened. Most people would think that they had a very good life. Me too.

***

In July, Alice and I go down to the cabin for a few days to fish. The Bermuda High is in ascendancy, and every afternoon thunderheads pile up over the lake, great puffy clouds that by late afternoon turn from whipped cream white to the color of a bruise. Usually there's a shower. It's oppressively hot, but the speckled trout are biting, so we don't care.

Alice has been going through the cabinets my father built around the top of the main room. Nothing of any value is ever left in the cabin because any year a hurricane might obliterate it. Somehow it has survived all those storms while some of the cabins nearby have been destroyed and rebuilt several times.

She hauls down a broken gasoline lantern, boxes of shotgun shells, a shotgun with a shattered stock, long underwear, an old thermos, a brand new dry bag. I remember when my father bought the dry bag, only a few months before the accident.

Alice finds the Avenue Foch photographs in the bag. Thirteen of them. We spread them out on the table. I pick them up, change the position of one with another. My hands are shaking, and I wonder if Alice notices. It's as if my father has suddenly stepped into the room with us.

"I'll bet he had them at the house," Alice says.

"And then he brought them out here," I say.

She doesn't even ask me why because she knows I don't know. I wonder where he kept them in the house. But I don't really know he kept them there. They could have been in the safe deposit box.

There are some pictures of a building, but there's no way to be certain that they are of the one on Avenue Foch. All the pictures are dark and cloudy, as if there were not enough light coming into the lens. I make out a picture of a man's boot, the wheel of a car, a lighter one that shows a patch of sky over the top of the building.

"That's when he started doing it," she says.

Her voice is excited, as if she's made some sort of discovery in those clumsy indecipherable pictures. To me each one is a palimpsest. And I know that I'm never going to be able to interpret what's written there.

"Yes," I say. "His method. He never changed."

Alice is certain that he shot pieces of the building and a soldier's boot, and a car tire deliberately. All the others too, which are just like them. But I'm not so sure. I can't decide if he had the camera hidden under his coat or in a book satchel or possibly he was just so unskilled that they came out that way. It could have been that those German soldiers stood around and watched him take them and just didn't care.

When we go home, we don't talk much about the pictures. We've exhausted everything we might say about them. The discovery, after all those weeks of anticipation, has been a disappointment. I put the pictures away in the top drawer of my dresser and expect I'll forget about them.

And that's exactly what I do. As the summer passes, I take them out a few times. We talk about them one morning for a few minutes when we wake early in the cabin on Christmas day to shoot ducks. I'm taking more pictures of my own now, even some nudes of Alice. But not in the manner of my father. I've shot her in the pirogue and sitting on the screened porch of the cabin. I think I'm becoming a capable photographer.

Spring comes and then it's summer again and the River Control Structure has survived another period of high water. The river still flows past New Orleans to the Gulf.

One morning in June over breakfast Alice announces to me that she wants to go camping in the mountains.

"I've been thinking about those pictures," she says.

"Which ones?" I ask.

"All of them."

"I can't take my father's pictures."

"I know. But there's some sort of connection that we're missing. I still don't understand why he took them out to the cabin. Why he hid them."

And then I realize that it's she who's become obsessed with the photographs, not me. I imagine her opening the dresser drawer over and over and taking them out and looking at them, trying to puzzle out some meaning. I feel a little jealous because after all I'm the one who has the most clear right to obsess about them. Now I even feel a little guilty that I haven't, particularly after all those years of trying to imagine what the photographs might be like.

She tells me that she wants to use the camping equipment in the attic. During those summers we slept in a Baker tent. It's one of those tents that looks like a shed. The open front is taller than a man and a fly extends another ten or twelve feet. My father liked the design of the tent because during the rainstorm that came almost every day in the mountains we could sit around under the fly. There was no door with mosquito netting built in. We slept on wooden cots under mosquito bars.

We haul the tents and cots and sleeping bags outside. Alice drapes the bags over the patio furniture. I set up the tent in the yard. It's in good condition. The canvas smells like wood smoke. Every night my father would lay a fire just beyond the end of the fly, mostly for fun. But there were some summer nights when it did get cold.

In those days, we usually stayed for two weeks. Alice and I plan on a week. We discuss whether to go to the places where my parents went and decide not to. They stayed in the Smokey Mountains National Park or places close to it. The campgrounds are going to be too crowded now. We study maps and decide on a stretch of national forest in North Carolina close to the town of Linville.

As we travel up from New Orleans, I recall those drives in the early seventies. My father never approved of air conditioning. We'd drive up out of that sweltering heat into the coolness of the mountains. I think about turning off the air conditioning a few miles out of Atlanta to relive that experience but decide against it. I don't even tell Alice what I'm thinking.

We set up camp at a national forest campground on a ridge above Sweet Creek. One of the feeder streams to Sweet Creek is Gingercake, and it's said to have brook trout in it. When I go to sleep that night, my cot pulled close to Alice's, I smell the scent of my father's pipe tobacco still embedded in the fabric of the bag. And as I lie there, Alice already asleep, I think I can smell the scent of him beneath the tobacco. I try to remember his smell when I hugged him and the stink of him when we hunted together at the cabin where hot water was saved for doing dishes, not bathing.

In the morning we fish Gingercake and do catch some small brook trout. At the confluence of Gingercake and Sweet, Alice catches a nice rainbow. That night we build a campfire and sit before it in the ancient camp chairs. The only other people in the campground are some mountain bikers. They wander over and ask questions about the tent.

The next day I start to take photographs of Alice. First we hike down into Linville Gorge, and I take pictures of her posed on the huge rocks that lie jumbled about on the streambed. I'm careful to always make her face a part of the composition of the photograph. We make love on the warm rocks. We're able to make loud and uninhibited love that night, because the campground is deserted.

I learn from the owner of the little store on the highway that the campground is not favored by the locals. A year ago a young boy wandered into the campground one morning and used a rifle to kill a college age couple camping there. The killer is in prison serving life without parole, but the mystique of his senseless crime lingers in the place. He bore no grudge against the couple. He didn't even know them. He just wanted to kill somebody.

Then I start to take photographs of Alice along Sweet Creek. It's a narrow creek, only twenty feet wide when we ford it the first time. Every now and then we see a fisherman or some backpackers. But mostly we have it all to ourselves. Several miles downstream the creek enters a gorge where there are several drops of more than a hundred feet. There's only a little water going over them. At the bottom of the drops are plenty of huge boulders to photograph Alice on. I arrange her on the rocks. She throws back her head and closes her eyes against the glare of the sun. I'm sure that these are going to be my best photographs.

The week draws to a close. It's been perfect weather. In the afternoons we hear the thunder rumbling off somewhere above the mountains and clouds slide back and forth over the face of the sun, but it never rains on us.

We're to leave on Monday. On Saturday night we finally get a storm. It rains hard all night. The tent leaks some toward the back, and a little creek forms between our cots, but we stay dry. In the morning the sky is perfectly blue and cloudless. When we hike down Sweet Creek, we find it has risen by almost a foot. At the first big drop, we discover what now can be called a waterfall. A thin sheet of water is falling over the lip and down into the pool below. We descend the trail into the gorge. I'm planning on taking more pictures of Alice on the rocks.

After I spend the late morning shooting her, we have lunch. The day has become oppressively hot. Alice takes off her clothes again and I do too, and we swim in the pool. The water is cold. When we swim close to where the waterfall is hitting the pool, we are pulled back and forth by powerful currents. Finally a current pulls us into an eddy next to the base of the cliff face. The waterfall drums into the pool a few yards from us. The eddy circulates us round and round several times until we pull ourselves out onto a flat rock. We're both cold, so we sit there for a time and bask in the sun like lizards until we're warm again.

"It's too bad we have to go home," I say.

"You can take pictures of me at home," Alice says.

She stands up and works her way across the rocks until she's behind the waterfall. She yells something at me, but I can't understand what she's saying over the rush of the water. Then she makes motions of taking pictures. I understand that she wants me to take pictures of her behind the waterfall. My camera is on the other side of the pool.

Then she works her way back across the rocks and joins me.

"It would make a great picture," she says.

"I don't have a telephoto lens," I say.

"You can swim over, stand on those rocks."

Not far downstream from the waterfall there are some rocks just beneath the surface.

"Put the camera in the dry bag and then swim over and stand up on the rocks," she says. "It'll be easy."

I don't think it'll be so easy but possible. I swim back across the pool and put the camera in the dry bag. Then I return and position myself on the rocks. Alice is sitting on the rocks in the sun. I suppose that it's cold behind the waterfall. The rocks are slick, making it difficult to stand up, but I finally gain good purchase and manage to stand. I take the camera out of the dry bag and leave the bag hanging on its strap around my neck. Alice climbs over the rocks again to take up a position behind the waterfall.

Through the sheet of water I can make out the outline of her body. I can see a breast. But I can't see her face. I think of how strange it might look to anyone coming to the trail to glance over the edge of the gorge and see a man with a camera in his hands appearing to stand on water while facing a waterfall. From certain angles it would probably be possible to see all or part of Alice. I think that I would almost rather someone come along the trail and discover us making love on the rocks beside the pool.

I see her face for a moment. She's yelling something at me. I look into the view finder to compose a picture. I see a breast, then a leg but her face is gone. And I think: *So, this was what it was like for my father.* I continue to search for her face, for more of her body, but there is just that breast. I see the nipple clearly, erect from the cold. I search for her face. Then, as I give in and start taking pictures of the breast, one after the other, I wonder if she knows what I'm doing. I take picture after picture. Then the roll is gone. Reloading is too complicated in my position.

For a moment I stand there looking at her. It seems to me that there's slightly more water now coming over the lip above, and she's now almost completely obscured. I look into the viewfinder again. She's gone. The water eddies about my feet. I'm cold. I know I'm going to take more of these sorts of photographs. I think of composing her over and over in the view finder, patiently taking shot after shot until one day out of the those shadowy ambiguous photographs, those pictures of Alice, a clear image of my father will emerge.

Dream Fishing

ONE evening as Paul Frene and his girlfriend Joyce were watching the news on PBS, Paul saw his ex-wife Audrey's name and picture come up on the daily list of the dead in Iraq. She was an officer in a transportation company of the South Carolina National Guard. Hers was not a death in combat but the result of some sort of traffic accident. They had been divorced for ten years.

He would never have expected Audrey to join the national guard. It came as a complete surprise. But that was something he found himself experiencing with women with whom he had serious relationships. He would suddenly discover things about their characters he had never anticipated. Usually it was something that brought an end to the relationship. His parting with Audrey had been amicable. Now the woman he once thought he loved was dead. Or maybe he had never loved her. How could he love someone he did not really know? As soon as they separated, he found that he had no desire for any further contact with her. It was as if the marriage had never taken place. At the same time, the ease of the separation made him slightly anxious.

He was certain he loved Joyce. She had recently moved out of her small apartment and into his house in Charlotte, which he had inherited from his mother. And he wondered if Joyce would think less of him after sitting there watching the other names and pictures scroll by on the screen and realizing he had not shed a tear over the death of a woman who had been his wife for two years.

"I'm sorry," Joyce said.

"It's like it's the picture of a stranger," he said. "Someone I've met and I've recognized the name, but that I really hardly know at all."

Joyce made them double gin and tonics, and they talked about a chamber music group she had recently joined. Audrey's name did not come up again. Then they went to bed and made love. Afterwards, as he lay on his back beside her, he considered whether Joyce wondered if he had been thinking of Audrey while they made love. He had not, but now he was. He lay there for hours, replaying the scenes of their life in his mind: picnics, football games, a trip to Mexico. Unexpectedly he felt a sense of despair, a heaviness in his soul. And he wondered if he was grieving for something indefinable as much as for her, or possibly the source of his anxiety was the prospect of a life with Joyce. She was thirty-seven. He was a few years older. They had never talked about children. Did he want children? He was not sure.

He recalled that the last time he saw Audrey was about ten years before at a football game in Columbia. She was with a man and he had shaken hands with him and hugged Audrey. He could not remember the man's name. He was not sure if she had remarried.

Paul was an engineer at a nuclear reactor just over the state line in South Carolina and Joyce played the viola for the Charlotte Symphony, an unlikely job for a woman who had been raised in the North Carolina mountains. Hers was a musical family, her mother and father both country music performers on a modest scale. When Joyce was a child she had started taking viola lessons from a woman who had played with the New York Philharmonic. Her teacher had developed arthritis in her hands early in her career and so left New York to live in a house in the mountains. Joyce had gotten herself out of those mountains and into the Indiana School of Music.

Finally in the early hours of the morning he dropped off to sleep, no closer to any understanding of death or love than when he first lay listening to the regular sound of Joyce's breathing and began to think of his life with Audrey.

***

At breakfast they learned from the morning paper that her death was the result of collision of her Humvee with a tank, her careless driver at fault.

"Do you want to talk about her?" Joyce asked.

"No," he said. "I haven't seen her in a long time. There's nothing to talk about. She's gone."

He had no desire to go to her funeral. Joyce seemed to understand about that.

"Audrey wouldn't like that picture," he said.

"Oh, I think she looked cute in that helmet," Joyce said. "Not everyone can look cute in a helmet."

Paul knew Joyce's comments were sincere, because she was not a woman given to jealously. They were both thinking about getting married, had even discussed it. Paul was not sure why she was cautious. On his part he kept waiting for that hidden side of her to emerge that would make a life with her impossible. Things had appeared that he found surprising but not disturbing, no reason to break things off. Joyce grew belladonna among her roses. She processed the plant, the end result a fine powder, and then, when she was not engaged to play a concert, she dissolved a carefully measured amount of powder in a glass of sweet tea. The drug's effects could be unpredictable, and she had learned to be careful. She considered using this sort of drug a part of her mountain heritage. Her grandmother had been renowned as a local healer. Joyce had hinted that she mixed the belladonna with mountain herbs her grandmother had taught her to gather.

After drinking the potion she would go lie in the hammock in the back yard under the pecans. It produced mild hallucinations that she said put her in touch with herself. She quoted Schopenhauer to him, explaining it was necessary to find a way to make the Will stand motionless, so she could contemplate her music. But she never played, like some jazz musicians, and what seemed to him to be an almost obligatory practice for rock stars, under the influence of any drug.

In the past she had taken LSD and other hallucinogenic drugs but finally settled on belladonna.

"Maybe it was just the name," she told him. "I suppose that's what got me interested. Without it, playing for me is just not the same. It's what takes me the most out of myself. When I play, and it can be weeks later, I hear the music in a different sort of way."

He had once smoked some marijuana when he was a student at the university, but he had stayed away from more serious drugs.

"You're sure you don't want to go?" she said. "I'll go with you."

Audrey lived in Charleston and was to be buried there.

He was pleased that she offered and told her so. But he had not changed his mind about going to the funeral.

Later, as he drove to work and the cooling towers by the lake came into view, he felt refreshed, as if he had slept ten hours instead of four. He looked forward to the day, expecting that Audrey's death would produce no more sleepless nights.

***

Audrey was killed in early May and in early June, Joyce's father died after a long illness. Her mother had died when Joyce was in high school. At the funeral in the mountains, the tiny frame church filled with relatives. There were testimonials, weeping, and wild music—all completely foreign to anything Paul had experienced in the Episcopal church. The one familiar event was when Audrey played Mozart on her viola. She looked calm and absorbed while she played. She cried afterwards.

They spent the night in her parents' house and planned to drive back to Charlotte the next day. In the morning he woke not long after daybreak to discover Joyce was gone. He got out of bed and walked through the house looking for her. Then he went out onto the deck. Below was the rush of the creek, whose sound had been in his ears as he drifted off to sleep. The creek flowed through the fifty acres of hardwood forest that now belonged to Joyce. Joyce's father had done well with his surveying business.

He called Joyce's name but received nothing but the rush of the creek in reply. He could see a piece of it and the blaze of rhododendrons in bloom along the banks. Here and there patches of morning fog lay on the surface of the water. Everything smelled alive and wet in that riot of green, and he wondered why he had chosen to live in the city and not some place like this.

Then he saw Joyce wading across the creek carrying a fly rod in one hand. A canvas creel was slung over her shoulder. He called to her, and she waved back as she came out of the creek and climbed the slope to the stairs that led up onto the deck.

She ascended the stairs and then was standing before him. She was smiling, her face radiant. She took the creel off her shoulder and opened it for him to see. Inside were four brook trout, their colors still vivid.

"I've been wanting a mess of specs for breakfast," she said. "I caught them with flies Daddy tied."

"He would've liked that," he said.

"It was a good way to think about him," she said. "Oh, I wish you and Daddy could have fished together."

He remembered her father as a tall, frail-looking man who was connected to a portable oxygen tank by a plastic umbilical cord. Sometimes he carried the tank out onto the deck and played his guitar. He played for them the one time Paul visited with Joyce.

"Yes," he said. "That would have been good."

They talked about fishing as they ate the trout for breakfast.

"When did you last trout fish?" she asked.

"Not for a long time," he said. "And only a couple of times. I was never very good at it. I was always getting hung up in the rhododendrons."

"These little mountain creeks are tight."

She looked down at the stream.

"Once this was a good brook trout stream," she said.

She went on to explain how she did not expect brook trout to last much longer in her stream. There were too many brown trout. Her father had tried to persuade the game and fish people to come kill everything in the stream and start over. That was what they were doing in the Smokey Mountains National Park, whose boundary bordered her land. The park biologists killed off all the fish in a stream in sections above water falls. That way the browns and rainbows, artificially introduced into the streams in earlier years, could not again take over the stream from the smaller brook trout. The creek below the house was not really suitable for this restocking tactic, because there were no big drops or waterfalls until the stream was almost at the top of the mountain.

"Over in the park there's some big specs that'll strip line off a reel. I know some of those places. Maybe we'll go up sometime."

He told her that he would like that. He had never thought of her as a fly fisherman. This was the sort of discovery he liked to make. He found himself wondering if she would want to get married in the little church.

Then they shut up the house and drove back to Charlotte.

***

The next Sunday, Joyce spent the entire afternoon in the hammock, engaged with belladonna. She ate bagels and drank sweet tea. He refilled the pitcher once for her. She looked up at him and smiled and said nothing. She never told him when she was going to take one of her belladonna holidays. And she never talked about what she had experienced.

At breakfast the next morning she looked particularly refreshed and calm although she had a busy day ahead of her.

"Daddy's passing was hard," she said. "But I sure enjoyed having those brook trout for breakfast."

"We could go to the mountains next weekend," he said.

"I want to eat fish *you* caught, here at this table."

Then she produced her father's fly rod.

"Daddy built this rod himself," she explained. "It's just right for those little creeks. You'll need to practice roll casts in the yard. No room for a back cast."

He was not quite sure what she intended, why she was making this request. Was he to take the place of her father?

"You mean you want me to drive up and come back the same day?" he asked.

"Yes, we can eat what you catch for breakfast," she said. "A night in the refrigerator won't hurt them at all. Daddy liked to say that even on the hottest day in July a spec will keep in your creel better than any rainbow."

She told him she liked the idea of his bringing fish from the mountains for them to eat. She had a dream while lying in the hammock of his hooking and landing a big brook trout.

"I should fish in your stream?" he said.

"No, you won't catch any specs there," she said. "I don't know how I did. Nobody has caught them there for years. That morning was like a gift from God in memory of Daddy. You'll have better

120

luck in the park, on one of those streams they restocked."

"But it's illegal to keep brook trout in the park."

"I know. I dreamed it all afternoon, you catching fish in the park and us eating them. I've got to trust the dream."

So here it is, he thought. *That part of her that's going to make our being together impossible.*

"The company is not going to appreciate it if one of their engineers is caught poaching trout," he said.

"You won't get caught," she said. "I know the ranger. I know the woman he's seeing. You'll fish while they're in bed. You get caught by Tobias Carter, you just mention how you know all about him spending every Saturday afternoon in Helen Morgan's trailer. His wife would be pleased to know about that. To keep you quiet he'd let you poach every trout in the stream."

He found himself agreeing to do it at least once. Maybe that would satisfy her. He again wondered what strange link all this might have with her father's death. Or some tortuous connection with the relationship between the locals and the federal government. They still bore resentment about the park where they once freely hunted, running their hounds after bear, and fished, taking as many as they wished, and gathered ginseng and other medicinal herbs.

That evening, when he returned from work, he assembled the fly rod and tied one of her father's flies to the leader. Then he cut off the hook with a pair of pliers and went out into the yard to practice. He stood with his back to the hedge that ran along one side of their yard and practiced roll casts. It would be a struggle to keep the fly out of the rhododendrons on streams only a few feet wide.

He heard her car pull into the drive and then the sound of the door shutting. She had returned from playing at a funeral with her chamber music group. Her heels clicked on the concrete, and she came out onto the patio.

"Show me," she called.

He made a perfect roll cast, one of the few he had made that day.

She clapped her hands and shouted: "Bravo! Bravo!"

Then she disappeared into the house and he practiced casts until it was almost dark and there were bats twisting in the air above his head. He reeled in the line and walked across the grass toward the lights of the house.

***

He woke early Saturday morning and left the house while Joyce was still sleeping. It was a two hour drive to the section of the park where the creek was located and then he had to walk five miles to reach it. Joyce had told him that it was one of the first creeks they had restocked. The brook trout, unhindered by competition from the browns and rainbows, had grown to a good size. It was also a creek not often fished. For some reason there were more rattlesnakes than usual in the area and they liked to lie on the trails. The creek was like a staircase for a giant up the side of the mountain, with a pool at the bottom of each step. Joyce had given him directions and they had located the creek on a topographic map he carried with him.

"You watch for snakes on the trail," Joyce cautioned. "And don't you fish too late. I don't want you falling asleep at the wheel."

By late morning he reached the creek. There were signs posted warning that all brook trout had to be released. He had not seen another person and no rattlesnakes on the trail. There were lush growths of ferns among the rocks. The creek's banks were dense with rhododendron thickets, the bushes no longer in bloom.

He assembled the rod and tied on one of her father's flies. He threw her father's creel over his shoulder. Then he entered the water. He had brought a pair of felt-soled wading shoes. For weeks

122

it had been warm enough to fish without waders. He was wearing camouflage. He planned to take her advice and approach each pool slowly and at a crouch.

Almost immediately he had a strike, a good-sized brook trout, but he failed to set the hook. The fish had risen partly out of the water, and he saw the flash of its colors. At the next pool he immediately hung the fly on a rhododendron while trying to make a cast under an overhanging branch. He spent some time retrieving the fly and then tying on a new tippet—slow work because of the necessity of tying unfamiliar knots. By the time he approached the third pool he was hungry. He found a huge boulder covered with moss and ate his lunch there. He had packed three bottles of beer in his creel. He drank one with his lunch and put the creel in the stream to keep the others cool.

He felt sleepy. He made a pillow out of his fly vest, once the property of Joyce's father, now filled with the scent of his own sweat, not the dead man's, and lay down, pushing his cap over his eyes. When he awoke, he planned to fish hard until late in the afternoon. Immediately he dropped off to sleep, lulled by the rush of water over a drop.

When he awoke it was to the sound of a human voice. He opened his eyes and saw a park ranger standing over him. The nametag on the man's uniform read CARTER.

"Doing any good?" the ranger asked.

"Mostly catching fish in the trees," he said.

He wondered why Tobias Carter was not at this moment in Helen Moran's trailer. What had gone wrong? He saw from his watch that he had been asleep for three hours.

"What you got in that creel?" Tobias asked.

"Beer," he said. "Only way to keep it cool in this hot weather. Want one?"

"Can't, I'm on duty. Care if I take a look?"

Tobias picked up the creel and examined the contents. He held up a bottle of beer.

"Nice and cold," he said.

Paul kept expecting the ranger to examine his fishing license, but he never did.

"Good luck," the ranger said as he left. "Watch for them rattlesnakes. Lots of folks don't fish here because of them. You know about them?"

"Yes, he said. "I know."

He watched the ranger climb up the bank of the creek and then disappear along the trail.

It was almost time to start the hike back to the car. He decided to fish one or two more pools. It would be dangerous to keep fish with the ranger about, but at least he could practice catching them. In the first he failed to hook another brook trout. In the second he hung his fly in the overhanging branch of a hemlock, fifteen or twenty feet above the stream. He was forced to break the tippet and leave the dead man's fly hanging in the tree. Discouraged, he hiked out and made the drive back to Charlotte.

Joyce did not seem disappointed when he came home without any fish.

"It's hard to catch those wild trout," she said. "Particularly during a dry summer when the water's low and clear. But you'll get better. Next Sunday morning we'll be eating trout for breakfast."

She was, of course, surprised at his encounter with Tobias Carter. She immediately got on the phone.

"Well, his wife caught him," she said. "Now he's sleeping at the ranger station. He'll have plenty of time now to do his rangering. But don't you worry. He probably won't be back at that creek until next summer. I know Tobias. He is not a persistent person."

"What about the woman in the trailer?" he asked.

"Helen, well she found somebody else, some man who plays

the guitar," she said. "She went off with him to Nashville. That's where lots of folks go to play the guitar. And be disappointed."

***

The next three Saturdays he went up to the creek. But he had yet to land a fish. He was losing her father's flies at such a rate that he quit using them and began to buy his own. He had several long discussions with the owner of the fly fishing store in Charlotte over the best flies and tactics for brook trout. On each Saturday he spent a good portion of the afternoon asleep on his favorite rock. He had not seen a single rattlesnake. Tobias Carter had not made another appearance.

Then it was August and the region was in the grip of a severe drought. At breakfast one morning Joyce suggested that he take belladonna.

"It makes me play the viola better," she said. "It seems to me that it could help you to fish better. You're up in the trees all the time aren't you?"

He admitted that he was, unwilling to tell her that he was sleeping away some of the best time for fishing.

"How will it affect me?" he said. "It could be dangerous."

"You'll be taking half what I take," she said. "That's the dose I started with. It's never taken me to a bad place. It'll help. There are parts to fly fishing that are just like playing the viola. Take next Saturday off and try it. Give those fish a rest."

***

After lunch the next Saturday, he lay in the hammock and sipped the glass of sweet tea she had prepared for him. Then the glass was empty, but he felt nothing unusual. She was practicing in the house, the sweet mellow notes of the viola leaking out into the yard to mingle with the sounds of the mockingbird and cardinals.

125

The hallucinations began when he was watching a mockingbird in the bird bath a few yards away. When the bird shook itself in the water and the individual drops flew from its feathers, they suddenly slowed down and he saw that each drop was filled with rainbows and then he was inside each drop and then he saw the bird's heart pumping and he was inside the bird as it burst into song and he realized that he was the individual notes of the song. He knew that Joyce was still playing, but he was no longer distracted by the sound of the viola. He knew the sound was still there, but he was completely taken up with the life in the yard: insects flying and crawling, the slow solitary progress of a mole, the songs of the birds, the communal life of ants and bees. He saw everything at once. It was astonishing but not frightening.

And he was certain that he would see the creek in the mountains differently now. Even polarized glasses had not allowed him to really *see* into those pools. Joyce had been wrong. It was not about technique at all, not the movement of the bow across the strings of the viola or the way he moved his wrist to manipulate the rod. It was about seeing. He was confident that he would no longer spook brook trout lying at the foot of a pool and watch them dart away through the clear water. He would know exactly where they were.

It was evening when he felt separate again from the songs of the birds. Chimney swifts were swooping low over the trees. Joyce came out across the grass with two drinks in her hand.

"I can't hear the bird songs in the right way anymore," he said. "Is that what happens to you?"

"Yes, that's the way it should be," she said.

She handed him the drink.

"It's gone out of you now," she said.

They sat together on the hammock and had the drinks together. He wished he could make love to her in the hammock, but the neighbors were too close. Besides, mosquitoes were beginning to appear.

"I can't understand where these mosquitoes are coming from," he said. "It's been so dry. Doesn't seem like there'd be any place for them to breed."

"Yes, it's a mystery," she said.

They sat in silence for a time and slapped at mosquitoes.

"It will have an effect," she said. "Believe me. Next Saturday it will be different."

"I believe you," he said.

Was that what his life with her was going to be like, belladonna in a hammock? What else would emerge that he did not know about her? And for the first time he considered there might be things about him that might not suit her. What must it be like for a musician to live with an engineer who had no creative life at all?

He looked forward to making love that night. But after dinner he felt so fatigued that it was all he could do to shower and crawl into bed. He heard her moving about the room, but he was asleep when she came to bed. He slept long and deeply and did not dream.

* * *

The drought persisted, even in the mountains, when he drove up to fish the next Saturday. This time he left even earlier than usual. He wanted to give himself plenty of time. Joyce had encouraged him to fish until dark if necessary. If he felt too tired to drive home, he could spend the night in a hotel in Ashville.

As he began the hike to the creek, it was already uncomfortably hot. When he reached the waterfall, that barrier to the browns and rainbows, he decided to swim in the pool below the falls before he began to fish. As he was taking off his clothes, he saw a big brown trout rise in the center of the pool to take some insect. He made a surface dive at the point where the trout had risen and swam down deep in an attempt to get a look at it, but the water was too roiled for him to see clearly, and a powerful current quickly bore him away from the big trout's lair.

He sat on a sun-bathed rock beside the pool and let his body dry before putting on his clothes. Then he took the trail up and around the waterfall and began to fish. He quickly discovered that if a belladonna and mountain herb trip helped Joyce play the viola better, or made her believe she could play it better, it did not necessarily do much for his trout fishing. After all, she was already an accomplished player and any improvements would be subtle ones. He was a beginner who showed almost no aptitude for the sport.

At the first pool he did hook a fish, but his knot that connected the tippet to the leader was a poor one and came undone. The fish vanished into the pool, probably with the hook still in its mouth. He hoped it had not been deeply hooked. He took the time to go through his collection of flies and with a pair of pliers cut the barbs off all the hooks. This would make it harder to hook fish, but at least it would decrease the chance of a fish permanently carrying a fly in its mouth.

The next pool was especially promising. He had once seen a large trout in it. He made his approach on his hands and knees and, when he drew closer, on his belly. His eyes were fixed on the center of the pool so that it was just by chance that he glanced to one side and saw movement, not in the pool, but on a little patch of sand at the foot of pool. No more than ten feet away two big timber rattlesnakes were mating. Each well over six feet long, they lay together with their bellies against each other, making one double snake. One of them was shaking its rattle slightly, but he could not hear the sound it made over the rush of water.

He abandoned the pool to the snakes, and walked out of the creek and took the trail to the next one. This one he approached in exactly the same way, although he did scan the ground in front of him more carefully than he had done at the first pool. He made his first cast to the foot of the pool from a kneeling position and then carefully worked the fly over all the likely spots, ending his fishing in the foam and eddies created by the water falling from a three foot drop.

In this manner he ascended the mountain pool by pool. He fished carefully and only hung the fly in a hemlock once in three hours of fishing. Now he was beginning to think that his afternoon with belladonna might actually have had a good effect on the mechanics of his fly fishing. But he did not get a single strike. Perhaps the fish were so heat stressed, the water so low, that they had gone into a kind of hibernation at the bottom of the deep pools. Once he heard the grumble of thunder far away and saw a few dark clouds through the treetops, but the sound of the thunder moved away, and the sky became blue and cloudless again.

Now he had reached a part of the creek he had never fished. It bent away from the trail and went up a steeper section of the mountain. He paused and ate his third sandwich and drank his last bottle of beer. He considered taking a nap but decided that this day he would continue to fish as long as he could see the fly on the water.

As he ascended the creek it become considerably narrower, so that in places it was not possible to make any sort of normal cast. As he had been advised by the owner of the fly fishing shop, he fished with just the leader. He held the hook between his thumb and forefinger and pulled back the rod tip as he might have pulled a bow, and then released the fly, catapulting it away to land beneath overhanging rhododendrons only a few feet away.

But still no trout rose to the fly, no matter how skillful a presentation he made, no matter how promising the spot. Discouraged, he decided that he would pick what looked like a perfect pool and then watch it until he saw a fish rise. It was not long before he found it. The pool was long and narrow and no wider than a bathtub and at its deepest point, where the water fell over the upstream drop into it, the pool was no more than a foot deep. The water was perfectly clear, so transparent that in places it could have been air instead of water. On one side rhododendrons almost completely overhung the pool, which because of the drought had shrunken considerably, leaving a narrow beach of fine white quartz sand. It was already late in the afternoon and the beach was in shade as well as the entire pool, except for the head, where the falling water sparked in the sunlight. He made a pillow out of his fishing vest, and turned his eyes toward the pool. When a fish rose for a insect, he would fish that spot.

Instead of watching he fell asleep. He dreamed he was watching Joyce make love to Tobias Carter on the rocks in the stream, balanced together like a pair of acrobats. She knew he was watching because she turned and smiled at him. As he started to call out to her, to protest, he woke. He had slept for over an hour. The head of the pool was now in shade. Under the rhododendrons trout of a good size were rising for some unfamiliar insect.

From a kneeling position he began to cast under the rho-dodendrons. There was enough room to make a roll cast. The very first cast was perfect and he hooked a fish and felt its weight on the line. But then it threw the hook, and he was sorry that he had cut off the barb.

He stopped fishing and lay on the sand again to wait for the fish to start rising. In fifteen minutes they began again. This time his first cast landed in one of the overhanging branches. Unable to work it loose, he carefully pulled on the line and broke the tippet. By the time he had finished tying on a new tippet and fly the fish were rising again. Again his first cast went directly into one of the overhanging branches, and he was forced to break the tippet.

He could still see the pool clearly. As he held the new tippet he had just cut in his hands, he watched a fish rise for an insect in the center of the pool. He dropped the leader and for the first time in several hours stood on his feet. He cast no shadow on the water, for the sun had dropped behind the mountain. In the trees the birds were singing their evening songs.

Without really thinking what he was doing, he stepped into the pool. As he did he realized that he was going to catch the trout with his hands. It was possible in a pool so narrow and shallow. He wished he had a net, some sort of seine. But all he had were his hands. He walked up the pool at a crouch, splashing his hands in the water. Ahead he saw a fish dart away and then another, swimming for the slightly deeper water at the head of the pool.

It turned out to be easier than he had expected. On the first pass through the pool, he caught a plump trout, pinning it against a rock. It was with great satisfaction that he dropped it into his creel. Then he went to the foot of the pool again and repeated the process. It took only ten sweeps of the pool to put three more trout in his creel. By now it was too dark to see the fish. A bat twisted in the air above the pool.

He went back down the creek until he reached the section he had fished before and climbed the bank to the trail. He walked by flashlight back to the trailhead, scanning the trail before him for rattlesnakes. The night was their time for hunting.

***

It was just after midnight when he arrived home. All the lights in the house were on. He found Joyce watching a movie. He showed her the fish, their colors still brilliant.

"I knew you could do it," she said. "Making a cast was different, wasn't it?"

"Yes, it was," he said.

He had decided not to tell her how he caught them. He wondered if she would expect him to make more trips to the mountains or if this one successful trip would satisfy her.

While he cleaned the fish, she opened a bottle of champagne to celebrate. They watched the last fifteen minutes of the movie while they drank the champagne. She drank most of it. Then he took a shower and they went to bed.

"Make love to me," she murmured when he slipped into bed beside her.

"Why did you want me to fish?" he asked.

He recalled the flex of her father's rod in his hands, the weight the dead man's creel on his shoulder, the comfortable pressure of his fishing vest against the small of his back.

She giggled.

"Oh, I don't know," she said.

She put her hand on him.

"Next thing you'll have me take up the guitar," he said.

She did not reply.

As he ran his hands over her erect nipples, asking questions no longer seemed important.

Only afterwards when they lay together, her head on his chest, did he think of questioning her again.

"Joyce—" he began.

"Hush," she said and kissed him. "In the morning, after we eat those fish."

So he wrapped his arms about her and waited for sleep, eager for some dream that might speak to him of some secret part of her life, a place he suspected was going to remain hidden, buried so deeply that not even an entire life with her was likely to yield a satisfactory answer. But in the morning, when those hard-won fish were reduced to bones and bit of fin on their plates, he would speak to her, he would try.

The Poisoned Arrow

MY mother is dying. It is just after midnight, the day after the 4th of July, and people have finally stopped shooting fireworks. Earlier I stood at the window of her hospital room and watched the rockets going up out of the ugly brick buildings of the public housing development that lies just beyond the hospital's live-oak covered grounds. I was too far away to hear any noise through the window. I find myself wondering if there are more births than deaths in the early hours of the morning.

Even though my father died when I was very young, I have never been close to my mother. After my father's death in Mississippi, my mother moved to South Carolina where her favorite brother lived. My childless uncle took the place of my father. He died last year. All my mother's kin of her generation have died, their children scattered throughout the country. Some of the children will return for the funeral.

So it is just my girlfriend Sarah and I, bearing witness to my mother's passing from life to death. Sarah has one arm thrown over my shoulder. Our faces are turned not to each other, but toward the dying woman in the bed. The young doctor stands on the other side of the bed.

"Judson," my mother calls.

I find her voice surprisingly strong and clear. For some reason

133

I do not want to leave Sarah's embrace.

"Go to her," Sarah says.

I stand by the bed and take her hand. It feels cold, but the grip is firm. The young doctor steps back into the shadows. Taking her cue from him, Sarah does the same.

I think of those death-bed speeches so favored by Victorians. But I can recall only a single one, that of the painter Turner: "The sun is god." I do not expect anything of that sort from my mother.

"Come close," my mother says.

I bend over her, realizing she wants to whisper something to me.

"This is just between us," she says.

She smells like the hospital, her breath identical with the air in the corridors, that scent of cleanser and plastic tile. At her request they stopped feeding her two days ago. She has orchestrated her own death.

Sarah has expressed admiration. She said it was something she would have done, putting everything in order. Sarah came to Columbia two years ago with me. I thought she and my mother would like each other from the moment Sarah set foot in my mother's spotless house. Even though Sarah says I am hopelessly obtuse in such matters, it became immediately clear to me that they intensely disliked each other on sight.

I do not live my life like my mother or Sarah. My apartment and studio are always in disarray. I never balance my checkbook.

I wait for her to speak, my ear close to her mouth.

"I lied to you about your father's death," she said. "There was no accident. Pearl Spann killed him. In the Holiday Inn in De Soto. Stabbed him in the heart with a poisoned arrow. I'm sorry I lied to you."

I'm still jetlagged. Sarah and I have come from France to South Carolina. I teach design at an art school in Paris, and Sarah works for the *Herald Tribune*. I can not understand why my mother is saying this. And I wonder if it is the opiate talking, the morphine that at this moment is seeping into her body. The cancer has not attacked her brain, just practically every other organ in her body.

"What?" I say.

I see Sarah move out of the shadows and into the light. She knows something is wrong. I hold out my arm, my palm up and facing her, and she stops.

"Pearl killed him," she says.

"Why are you telling me this?" I ask.

She closes her eyes and sighs. Her body, tense with urgency a moment before, is relaxed and still. It is as if she has fallen into a deep sleep, but I know she is dead. The doctor knows it too. He steps out of the shadows and into the light. I suppose, after we are out of the room, he will put the stethoscope he wears around his neck to my mother's breastless chest. They were the source of it, removed by the surgeon, but it was already too late.

***

Sarah does not ask me any questions until we are in the car. I start to put the car in gear, but she puts her hand on mine.

"What's going on?" she asks. "What did she say to you?"

"Crazy things," I say.

"So tell me."

"Just crazy things."

"Tell me and I'll decide how crazy they are."

I'm glad Sarah is here. She is strong like my mother. My mother, after the death of my father, went back to school and became a lawyer at a time when very few women in the country were doing that.

I tell her the story I knew from childhood of my father's death, how he fell out of a tree stand while bow hunting for deer and impaled himself on the poisoned arrow nocked on his bow string.

Sarah expresses astonishment that he was hunting deer with poisoned arrows. I'm not a hunter. It was not until I was in high school that I did some reading and found out about the use of poison arrows by deer hunters. Before I did that the term "poisoned arrow" was enough for me, something out of accounts of explorers' exploits in the rain forests of Africa or South America.

I discovered it was legal to use poison arrows for deer in Mississippi at the time my father died. The poison rode in a pod just below the broadhead. When the arrow entered the deer, the pod burst. The poison made it impossible for the deer to breathe.

I was five years old when it happened. I remember little about the funeral. But I can clearly call up the image of my mother sitting alone at the kitchen table and crying. A few weeks after that we left for South Carolina.

Then I tell Sarah my mother's revelation.

"I don't believe it," Sarah says. "It's the morphine."

"Maybe," I say.

"Tomorrow we'll call the local newspaper," Sarah says.

Later, as I go to sleep, I try not to think about what my mother has told me. I find myself wondering if my father is even dead. Perhaps his death too is a fiction of my mother's making. I toss and turn and keep waking Sarah up. Finally she puts her arms around me and I sleep.

***

When I call the *De Soto Discoverer* in the morning, everything is instantly made clear, at least the veracity of my mother's revelation. No one has to look in files. Someone puts the publisher of the paper on the line. Morgan Allen tells me it is all true, that a woman named Pearl Spann killed my father at the Holiday Inn.

"So, Helen made up some story," he says. "I suppose she did it for you."

"Me?" I ask.

"It was a pretty bizarre way to kill a man. They don't usually do it that way. A gun. Sometimes a knife. You were too young to understand."

"I don't understand now."

"I wish I could come to the funeral."

"Columbia is a long way from De Soto."

"Look, don't you think badly of Helen for doing what she did."

"I don't. Tell me, why did that woman kill my father?"

"Love. Jealousy. It's all the same thing. Your father had promised he was going to leave your mother, marry her. At least that's what she told the jury. She was convicted of manslaughter. Went to Parchman for two years and then was paroled. And you know the strange thing, she came back here to live just like nothing had happened. Like she'd gone to Europe on vacation. She's still alive. Lives alone. Still runs her farm. She's a good farmer, better than most."

He then asks me questions about where I am living and what kind of work I do.

Over breakfast Sarah and I talk about my conversation with Morgan.

"Do you wish she hadn't told you?" Sarah asks.

I explain to her that my father has always been a shadowy figure, how my uncle took the place of my father.

"I don't know what I feel," I say.

Then we get caught up in the events connected with the funeral. A few of the children show up. None of my father's kin come. My father's people are from Fairhope, Alabama, just across the bay from Mobile.

My father came home from Vietnam and finished his

engineering degree at Auburn. Then he went to work for the Corps of Engineers at their research station in De Soto. He was not buried there but in his hometown of Fairhope. He and my mother, who was from Mobile, had known each other slightly when they were growing up. Then they rediscovered each other at Mardi Gras one spring and fell in love.

I have a memory of riding with him on a boat on the Mississippi and the captain letting me sound the horn and a towboat sounding hers in reply. Another is his map of the river. It was a long, narrow map of the entire length of the river. I can recall watching him unfold it in the big house we were renting on Main Street. The map stretched from one side of the house to the other. He had to throw open two sets of pocket doors to make space for it.

"Let's walk the river," he said.

Those are the only words of his I can now remember clearly. I wonder exactly what he said to Pearl Spann to make her plunge that arrow into his heart.

He took my hand, telling me to be careful and not step on the map, and we walked along the edge. He named important features, those names lost to me, but I do recall his reciting them. I can't even imagine what those names might be like.

Finally it is over; my mother is buried. I decide to return later, perhaps during the break between semesters or next summer, and clean out her house and put it up for sale. I arrange for someone to keep the grass cut and check on the place from time to time.

**

Sarah and I are having dinner together the night before we are due to return when I realize I must go to De Soto. I want to at least set eyes on the woman who killed my father. I know that Sarah can't go with me. She is scheduled to interview someone in Paris.

"I have to go to De Soto," I say.

"That's crazy," she says. "What are you going to do there? You know what happened now."

"I know my mother's version."

"Oh no, you're not going to try to talk with that woman?"

"Maybe I'll just ride by her house."

Sarah is so exasperated that she can only sigh. She orders dessert, something she hardly ever does. Then she orders coffee and drinks two cups. I expect that she will be up all night.

But as it turns out she is the one who sleeps soundly. I find myself sitting at her laptop in the hotel room, trying to find out something about De Soto. But beyond the material from the Chamber of Commerce, who are clearly willing to make any sort of bargain with any sort of company that will locate in the town, I find nothing. There is a Spann Avenue that runs off Main Street.

Sarah is calm when I drive her to the airport. I leave later that day for Mississippi. I am going to fly to Memphis and pick up a car there. I linger at security with her as we say our goodbyes.

"Judson, I never expected you would do something like this," she says. "I guess I'm disappointed."

"Disappointed," I say.

"Yes, you're not acting like an adult."

And I feel like we have just shaken hands instead of kissed. Then she is gone through the line, holding her shoes in one hand long before anyone is going to ask her to take them off. After she is past the machines and the searches, she turns and blows me a kiss before she heads for her gate.

***

It's unbearably hot in the Mississippi Delta. I drive down from Memphis on the two lane highway that runs the length of the Delta, pass seemingly endless fields of cotton, soybeans, and rice. Here and there along rivers and creeks are patches of woods, places where I suppose my father once hunted.

De Soto is a small town built beside the Mississippi River. The federal levee looms above it. There is the usual statue of the Confederate soldier leaning on his rifle and looking patient and reliable. There is also a statue of Hernando de Soto, the discoverer of the Mississippi, who came to the region seeking gold but found only wars with Indians. According to the plaque, he stumbled upon the Mississippi at a low bluff a short distance from the town. The town seems to be thriving. Only one building has plywood over what was once the plate glass window of a store front. The office of the *De Soto Discoverer* is located on Main Street. I noticed a sign for the Holiday Inn, also on Main Street, outside of town, but I have not seen it yet. Morgan and I are having lunch together.

I find Morgan Allen sitting behind a battered roll top desk in a tiny office at the rear of the newsroom. He is a man in his early sixties, about my mother's age. Before I get to ask him about the location of the Holiday Inn or where Pearl Spann lives, he tells me that he and Pearl Spann are exactly the same age. They went through school together.

"She was a beautiful girl," he said. "She's still beautiful."

I think of pictures of my mother when she was young. No one would consider her beautiful. She had trouble with her weight all her life and only grew slim again with the onset of the cancer.

"Might have married her myself, but then I met Lucy," he says.

He tells me we are going to lunch at the Holiday Inn.

"Don't you worry," he says. "It's new. The old one got blown away by a tornado."

We walk down Main Street. The Holiday Inn occupies what was once the shell of an abandoned hotel. For years a home for bats and possums, he says. A plaque points out it was used as a hospital and briefly as the headquarters of a Yankee general.

The dining room is painted with a mural depicting the discovery of the river, all the figures looking heroic. It is a fresco, done by some artist from California. Morgan tells me the artist had gone to Italy to study the frescos there and learn the technique.

"He put the faces of people from the town on the Spaniards," Morgan says. "I'm the priest."

I look more closely and see that the priest does have Morgan's face.

"The mayor is De Soto," Morgan says. "He's dead now. Got drunk and fell out of a duck blind last year and drowned. I wrote his obituary."

We both order stuffed flounder. We drink a couple of whiskies. I feel strange being here and think about Sarah's reaction to my coming.

While we are waiting for our food to arrive, Morgan begins to tell me about my father's death and the trial at the county courthouse.

"Oh, it was a circus," Morgan says. "There were reporters from Memphis and Jackson. The Spanns are important people here. The mayor was a Spann. I think he was one of Pearl's cousins."

"What happened in the motel room?" I ask.

"Your father had promised Pearl he would divorce your mother and marry her. They'd both had a few drinks."

He explains that my father took his bow, with its quiver of poisoned arrows attached, into the room.

"Why would he take a bow into the motel?"

"The prosecutor wondered about that too. He tried to make the case that Pearl went out to his truck and took the bow off the gun rack and while he was sleeping stuck one of those poisoned arrows into his heart. Pearl insisted that he had brought the bow into the room, that he was worried about it being stolen. I think the jury believed her. You know, your mother didn't come to the trial. She packed up and headed for South Carolina with you. I think

Pearl's attorney was glad about that."

Then he tells me about growing up with Pearl Spann and how well she could ride a horse and what a good shot with a pistol she was.

"I would've expected her to have shot him," he said. "She had a pistol in her purse, one of those little automatics ladies like to carry. But she chose the arrow instead. That was why I think the jury let her off on the lesser charge. I suppose not using the pistol implied she'd lost control and picked up the first weapon that was handy. Her attorney came down hard on that. 'Struck that blow in a fit of passion,' her lawyer kept saying. I think George Fairchild thought he was performing Shakespeare when he got up to defend a client."

We linger over lunch and get off the subject of my father and Pearl Spann. I end up telling him about teaching art in Paris, mostly to American students. He has been to Paris a few times. Then we walk back to his office where he gives me a folder containing his paper's coverage of the trial. He has also drawn me a map showing me how to find Pearl Spann's farm.

"To see her you'll have to go out there," he says. "She doesn't come to town much. If I were you, I'd just ride by her place. Or buy yourself a pair of binoculars and wait until she walks out the front door."

I tell him I will think seriously about his advice.

***

I check into the hotel and sit on the bed with the contents of the folder spread out before me. Pictures of my mother, my father, and Pearl. Morgan was right. She is beautiful. That is clear even in the grainy black and white newspaper photographs.

I read the stories, most of them written by Morgan himself. It turns out that my father intended to buy a boat, a fifty foot motor yacht, in St Louis, and had promised Pearl they would take it down the Mississippi together after they were married. He was going to quit his job with the Corps of Engineers. They would wander about the Caribbean. I wonder if my father's plans ever involved getting in touch with me again. If he had stayed with Pearl would I have spent my summer vacations on that boat?

There was nothing about exactly why he was leaving my mother other than Pearl's obvious attractions. Pearl spoke one sentence about it. "Sloan told me she was cold." Pearl did not offer any insight on why he had changed his mind, after he had taken out his savings to make a down payment on the boat. She offered no explanation other than passion and jealously for why she plunged the broadhead into his heart. She claimed she had been startled to see the arrow sticking in his chest and the bed filling with blood. But she did not claim to have been temporarily insane, just so enraged that she did not connect his death, at the instant the arrow was in her hands, with her subsequent actions.

According to Morgan's final article both the judge and the jury were sympathetic. There was one article from the *Commercial Appeal* suggesting that the judge or the jury had been tampered with by the Spann family, but in the ensuing investigation nothing like that was uncovered.

I read some of the articles twice and sit there and look at the picture of my father. I open the bar and make myself a vodka and tonic. I stand at the window and look at the grass-covered levee shimmering in the heat.

Then I take out the map and look at the picture of Pearl Spann. The house is located near the river, but not as close as the town. I suppose there are fields between the house and the levee. I still am not certain what I am going to do when I find the house. Do I drive up and introduce myself as the son of the man she killed? I had forgotten to ask Morgan if she is in good health, if she would be able to take the shock of an event like that. I decide it is a good idea to take Morgan's advice and buy myself a pair of binoculars, observe her from a distance.

I still feel jet lagged; I close the curtains and lie on my back on the bed and try to sleep. Finally I do, a deep sleep free of dreams. When I wake it is evening. I go down and have dinner in the restaurant, taking a table opposite the figure of the priest with the face of Morgan Allen.

Then I walk south on Main Street, searching for Spann Avenue, which I forgot to look for on my journey into town. I find it and turn left toward the river. As I walk past the big houses, I wonder which ones are still owned by Spanns. Then I go up onto the levee. Below there is a wharf where barges are being unloaded. I walk a little way on the gravel road atop the levee until the wharves are obscured by a stand of cypress. In front of me the river stretches away, more than a mile wide, to the Arkansas shore. The sun, the red ball of it looking like a picture in a travel agency brochure, is setting over the flat fields of the Arkansas delta. I think of my father and Pearl going down a river in that motor yacht, New Orleans and the islands of the Caribbean lying before them.

By the time I get back to the hotel I feel like sleeping, even though it is not close to being completely dark. I am thankful for that, because I imagined I might be up late, unable to sleep until the early hours of the morning. But after watching the news on TV, I fall asleep as I read over the newspaper articles.

***

In the morning I find an outdoor store where rifles and shotguns rest on racks and deer, boar, and bear heads are mounted on the walls. I buy a pair of binoculars intended for spotting deer. They are camouflaged. The salesman tells me they are coated with a special non-reflective paint to prevent a wary deer spooking by the flash of sunlight off them. I test them out on the levee, which is just a thin green line in the distance. When I put the glasses to my eyes, a herd of cows grazing on the side of the levee springs into view.

"You'll be ready with those," the clerk tells me. "Deer season'll be here before you know it. I got me a pair."

"I want to be ready," I say.

I follow the directions, driving out amid the fields of soybeans and cotton. Then I take a wrong turn and get lost and have to ask directions at a crossroads store. The clerk does not have any reaction at all to my announcement that I am searching for Pearl Spann's farm. She tells me I'm close and gives me directions. I don't really know what I expected. The clerk is in her twenties, the murder ancient history to her. Maybe she doesn't even know about it.

This time I make no wrong turns and find the farm. The landmark I am looking for is a tractor shed with a red roof. I see the bed of a blue pickup, the rest of the truck hidden behind a hedge. The house, a ranch style that would not look out of place in any suburb in the country, is located in a grove of pecans. Morgan told me the Yankees burned the original house during the war. A new house in classical style was built there later, but it too burned down. That time instead of federal troops it was faulty wiring. A driveway runs through the center of the grove to the house, perhaps a quarter of a mile separating the house from the highway. Far away across the fields behind the house, I can see the green smudge on the horizon that marks the levee.

I pull off the road by the mailbox and take out the binoculars. It is then I realize how exposed I am. But I decide to take at least one quick look at the house.

When I put the glasses to my eyes, the house springs into view. I see a pair of work gloves on the front steps and a tool that looks like a pair of pruning shears. I sweep the glasses across the yard around the house, searching for the owner of the gloves. I try the pecan grove and see only grass and trees.

Then I see the sun flash off something. I put the glasses on the spot. There at a window a woman is pointing a rifle at me. She is looking through a telescopic sight. I freeze and for a moment I'm not sure I can make my body move. Finally I duck down below the window, thinking as I do that the sheet metal of the car is not much protection from a bullet. At least she will not be sure exactly where I am in the car.

But no shot comes and I realize she wanted to take a look at me, not shoot me. After all I was looking at her, spying on her house. I ease my head above the window again and put the binoculars to my eyes. Now she is no longer holding the rifle. She is standing at the window waving at me.

Mason was right, she is beautiful. She has the perfectly proportioned face of a Greek statue. She is dressed in a blue short-sleeved work shirt and jeans and is wearing a turquoise necklace and matching earrings. Her blonde hair is pulled back and tied with a blue and white scarf. She smiles at me, displaying her perfect teeth, and motions for me to come up to the house.

I am not sure what I should do. I hadn't counted on this. But then I decide I won't tell her who I am. I will say I am a journalist who is revisiting the story, that I am interested in finding out from her what her life at Parchman was like. And as I drive toward the house, I improve my plan. I will say that I am doing a piece about women in Southern prisons.

She is out on the porch waiting when I arrive, standing with the gloves and shears in her hands. I get out of the car and walk across the gravel. Up in one of the pecan trees a blue jay is screaming at something: a squirrel or maybe a snake. I reach the porch and start to introduce myself with the name I have invented and to apologize for spying. But I do not get a chance.

"Sloan's child," she says.

146

My mother always claimed I looked like my father. I have never thought so. I stop, standing there on the gravel as if a water moccasin was coiled between us, and she had just warned me not to step on it.

"I am . . . ," I begin. "I mean, I'm sorry I disturbed you."

I know that is inadequate. But I don't know what else to say, and I have to say something. I can't seem to connect this woman with the pictures in the folder Morgan gave me.

"I'll make us some coffee," she says.

I follow her into the house and through the rooms decorated with pieces of Mayan pottery.

"I spent time in Mexico," she says. "In the winters."

I wonder if she has a lover in Mexico. I find myself momentarily arrested by this thought. I am not in the habit of imagining lovers for women in their sixties. But then the image of her riding horses with someone on a hill above the sea springs into my mind. I find myself becoming angry with this woman who, because she could not have my father, plunged an arrow into his heart. But the anger does not take the form of my wanting to shout at her or do her violence. I've never struck another person in anger. Although like my father I am a big man, I was never interested in playing violent sports. My skin suddenly feels prickly all over my body; I take several slow breaths to calm myself.

Then we are on a screened porch that looks out on a garden. I can't see the fields and the levee because of a tall, thick hedge that runs across the entire length of the yard.

She goes to make coffee. I think about bolting and running for the car.

And she, as if she knows what I am thinking, sticks her head around the corner of the doorway.

"You stay put," she says.

Then she disappears again and a few moments later returns

with the coffee.

"I saw your car sitting there by the mail box," she says. "We've had trouble with robberies. I'm sorry about the rifle."

"What if I'm not who you think I am?" I say.

She pauses for a moment.

"You could be nobody else," she says. "It's as if Sloan were sitting right there in that chair."

She pauses again and sighs and takes a deep breath before she speaks.

"I'm going to tell you exactly what happened," she says. "I'm not going to tell you any lies. Remember that it's been a long time, and the girl who killed your father doesn't exist any longer. She might even try to make some sort of excuse. Even tell lies. God, I wish I'd been compelled to do it, that Sloan had threatened me. But that's not true. He was a gentle man. A good man. Now listen."

What she tells me is the same story I heard from Mason.

"I just lost control," she says. "It was like I was watching someone else take that arrow off the bow. And I've often thought if he hadn't brought the bow into the room it wouldn't have happened."

I wonder if she remembers she had the pistol in her purse. And I try to imagine them together in the motel room, but I find it impossible. I just can't see this woman with a poisoned arrow in her hands.

"It went in so easy," she said. "It made me think for a moment that it hadn't happened at all, that I could just pull it out and it would all be undone. Your father didn't suffer. I have thought of your father every day since. I wake up in the morning thinking of him."

She pauses for a moment and takes a deep breath.

"I wish I'd driven that arrow into my own heart."

She puts her hand over her heart. I can see that she is having trouble controlling herself. There are tears in her eyes. But then she masters herself and I find myself admiring her. At the same time I wonder if she actually does think of my father when she wakes in the arms of some lover in Mexico.

"Your mother was destroying him, you know," she says. "I mean, it wasn't something she planned to do. Sloan was a passionate man. She wasn't."

"My mother," I say.

"Yes, her. Your father had promised. We were going to visit all the islands. And then he was dead and I was in Parchman. But I guess I haven't explained anything you didn't know."

I start to speak. I want to speak.

"Could I have more coffee?" I ask.

"You like it?" she asks.

"Very much."

"I order it directly from New Orleans."

She gets up to refill our cups. I decide that I'm going to drink one more cup of coffee and then leave. I can't recall any time in my life when I have felt more uneasy.

When she is gone for much longer than would be necessary to fill the cups, I again think of getting up and walking out the door and pretending to myself that I never came here at all. Then I hear her footsteps. She is carrying not coffee cups but a stack of paper.

"This was your father's," she says.

As she starts to unfold it, laying it out on the table between us, I realize it is the map of the river. She has unfolded the bottom section where the river empties through the Passes into the Gulf. She puts her fingertip on the map and moves it past the mouth of the river.

"We were going out there," she says.

She fixes her eyes on the map as if she is imagining them taking the yacht down through one of the Passes. We are both silent. The jays are still venting their displeasure upon something out in the yard. She looks up at me.

"Oh, I shouldn't have asked you into the house," she says. "But you look so like Sloan."

Then I can see she is trying to say something.

"I can't—" she begins.

She looks down at the map again. She is trembling. I wonder if she is reliving that scene in the motel. Or perhaps she is thinking of standing beside my father as he steers the boat through the tropical night, the stars bright and clear scattered across the sky, the sea shining with phosphoresce.

Her gaze turns from the map to me. I notice for the first time that she has green eyes. She struggles to speak again but no words come out.

"Pearl," I say.

I wonder if she can hear me as she wanders about in that dream of what might have been.

"Pearl," I say. "I don't blame you."

We both stand there while I wait for her to speak. I hear the sound of her fingertips on that thin paper, now moving in the empty space which is the Gulf. It is an unnerving sound. I wonder what she is trying to discover there in that blank space. Then she stops and folds up the map carefully.

"You don't blame me?" she says.

"No," I say.

I don't know if that is even true. I am saying things without considering what I am saying. And maybe it is true. What I know is true is that I can't imagine this woman plunging that arrow into my father's chest.

I wonder how many times she has traced with her fingers their journey down the river that never happened.

"Take it," she says.

She thrusts it into my hands. I hold it tightly to keep it from unfolding and spilling out onto the table between us.

"Now go," she says.

I don't protest. I want to go; I want to get out of that house and away from her. We walk through the house and out onto the porch. The jays are silent. A mockingbird is singing from some hidden perch, high in the top of one of the pecans.

I'm at the bottom of the steps when I turn. She is standing on the porch. There is a fragility to her that I hadn't noticed before. Right now she looks as fine boned and delicate as a young doe. When I start to speak she puts a finger over her lips. I turn and walk to the car. I don't look back. But when I start down the driveway I turn my head, expecting to see her still standing on the porch. It is empty.

***

In the early hours of the morning I sit in my hotel room leafing through the contents of the folder. I'm not certain I will be able to sleep at all, and I'm concerned about the early drive to Memphis. I can imagine myself falling asleep at the wheel, coaxed drowsy by the monotony of those immense fields, the car sliding off the highway and coming to rest in someone's cotton field.

I pick up the map again. I decide I'll look at it and then try to sleep. As I unfold it, I quickly discover I want to see it laid out in its entirety. Again I remember the baritone of my father's voice and the words, "Let's walk the river."

I take the map out into the corridor and walk to the far end to give myself plenty of space. I imagine at this hour I'm the only guest awake in the entire hotel unless somewhere a couple is making love.

The map starts at St. Louis. So it is not a map of the entire river as I had thought all those years, but just of the lower Mississippi. I begin to read the names printed on the map, but they call up no remembrance of my father's recitation. Then below Memphis I see names written in what I am sure is my father's hand. They are of landings, plantations, points, bars, islands, and cutoffs. I realize that my father has superimposed names from some steamboat pilot's map, names of places that perhaps had vanished with the building of the levees and the straightening of the river by means of steel and earth and concrete. I wonder if he planned to give Pearl Spann some sort of historical tour as they made their leisurely way downriver.

First I read silently, my lips moving over the syllables, but as I pass Vicksburg I begin to say the names out loud: Catfish Bar, Cote's Creek Point, Hole in the Wila. Suddenly I hear my father's voice saying that name. A duel fought on a big sandbar. I remember him speaking of that. A big sandbar where we could hunt for turtle eggs. But that is all. I remember nothing else. Perhaps he was planning to take me down the river.

I continue my survey of the map again: Fairchild's Island, Chicot Landing, Dead Mans Rena, Ruths Hard Times. And this litany of names becomes a sort of prayer for my father. But I discover it gives me no comfort. I arrive at the Passes below New Orleans covered with sweat and despairing of any sleep this night.

The Oldest Man
in Mississippi

LUTHER Hart was summoned to Jackson, not by a phone call or an e-mail but by letter. The letter was written with a fountain pen on beautiful thick paper in the sort of graceful flowing hand people learned to write in the nineteenth century. As Luther finished the last sentence: *My boy, you will be expected to do your duty and come down here.* the word "summoned" came into his mind. He would not have been surprised if the closure was something like "Your obedient servant" or some such nineteenth century formality. But it was not. Instead his father had written: *Your father (the oldest man in Mississippi).* There was also a post script. *Come down here and I'll teach you how to live to be a hundred.*

He did not expect that his father was really the oldest man in Mississippi, but he was certainly *one* of the oldest. His father was turning one-hundred and the purpose of the letter was to invite Luther to his birthday party. Luther was to be the only guest. The letter had been perfectly clear about that.

Luther had not seen his father in years. If his father could be accused of indifference, Luther was not without blame. His father had been living in Mississippi for the last ten years; he could have made an effort to visit. He had used as an excuse for not going that Mississippi was a place full of racists. If his father had lived

153

in California it would have been easier, Luther told himself, to contemplate a visit. He was aware that there were other deeper and more complex reasons for staying away, but he did not want to think about them.

The last time Luther had seen his father had been at Luther's sixth birthday party. They were living in Houston. Luther had a photograph taken at the party. Dressed in a cowboy outfit, complete with chaps and wearing a brace of pistols at his waist, he was seated on a pony. His father, dressed in a seersucker suit, a Panama hat set at a jaunty angle on his head, and a cigar clenched between his teeth, was holding the bridle. He imagined that his mother was standing off to one side. They had still been married then. Sometimes Luther thought he could smell cigar smoke when he looked at the picture.

He was the only child from his father's last marriage. The old man had married Luther's mother when he was seventy years old. She had died last year of breast cancer. She was only in her early fifties. That Tillman Hart could father a child when he was seventy seemed to Luther an almost biblical feat. His father had never shown any particular interest in Luther before, although he usually remembered his birthday, probably, Luther guessed, because he was his last child, the sort of achievement he could brag about to his friends.

Luther, who had just turned thirty, worked as an investment banker in New York and made an excellent living at a job he enjoyed. He had from time to time considered that if he were lucky he might live at least as long as his father. After all he had never been sick a day in his life. To stay in shape he swam twice a week and played squash and court tennis. He never lacked for female attention, for he was a good looking man. He was not planning on getting married for a long time, maybe never. Why should he, he told himself, risk ruining a perfect life?

154

***

The next Saturday, after rising early and doing some work on his computer, Luther flew down to Mississippi. Actually his father's birthday was not until the next Wednesday, but his father had chosen Saturday to celebrate it, no doubt, Luther thought, to make it harder for him to refuse to come. He picked up a rental car at the small airport, to which the city had hopefully added the name "International," and drove into the city. There had been an article, in the *Times*, he thought, about how the city was in a state of siege from its poverty-stricken black population. The mayor had declared a curfew. Now it was the middle of July. People without air-conditioning would find it difficult to sleep on those humid Mississippi nights, the air as warm as a bath. So if you were young and poor you might go out and roam about and get yourself into trouble, maybe kill someone.

His father, who owned a printing company, one of his many businesses, had told him in the letter that he lived in an apartment in the printing company office. The plan was for Luther to spend the night there with his father and fly back to New York on Sunday. He wondered if it were possible to buy the Sunday *Times* in Jackson. His father had enclosed a map, drawn in ink with precision on the same thick paper. A compass was drawn in the upper right hand corner. The printing company was in the southwest section of the city, next to a set of railroad tracks. He imagined his father drawing on the map a picture of the north wind, a wild-haired man with his cheeks puffed out, and populating the margins with fanciful monsters in the manner of the old cartographers.

The printing company was located in a section filled with warehouses near the railroad tracks. Paint was peeling on the façade. Vines loaded with bright red flowers climbed up one side next to the door. Grass and weeds grew out of cracks in the sidewalk and along the edge of the building. Next door was a newspaper office, JACKSON PRESS SCIMITAR painted in black letters on the plate glass window. When he got out of the car into the mid-afternoon heat, he noticed a hole in the window, the glass spider webbed around it. He was not familiar with such things, but he guessed the hole could only have been made by a bullet. He tried to recall the last time he had seen on TV a plate glass window with a bullet hole in it.

He noticed a bald man seated at a desk just inside the window. The man waved to him. He hesitated for a moment and then waved back. Luther hoisted his overnight bag over his shoulder and walked up onto the sidewalk. Inside the bag was a bottle of the most expensive Scotch he could find, his birthday gift to his father. His cell phone was in his pocket, turned off. He had decided to get through the weekend without it. The weeds had a rank smell. One clump rose taller than his head. It seemed hotter than New York even though the weather report had predicted identical highs and humidity for the day.

He walked to the door of the printing company. SAUNDER PRINTING was painted in black letters on the window. He wondered if the same sign painter had done both jobs.

"Mr. Hart," a voice called.

The man from the newspaper office was walking toward him on the sidewalk.

"Are you Mr. Hart?" the man asked.

He said he was and then the man, whose face was lined and puffy from age and possibly drink, was shaking his hand and introducing himself as Chester Raines. Chester, Luther thought, who looked like he was in his late forties or early fifties, was old enough to be his father. Luther found himself imagining normal fathers for himself from time to time.

"Your daddy'll be back after awhile," Chester said. "Your daddy is a fine man. An amazing man." Chester hesitated for a moment as if he had suddenly recognized how foolish this journey into hyperbole was making him look. "The door is open. Just go on it. His apartment is way in the back. He said you should make yourself at home."

When Luther made no move for the door, Chester stepped into the doorway and turned the knob and pushed it open.

"Go on in," Chester said. "It's all right."

"He leaves it unlocked?" Luther asked, thinking of the mayor's curfew.

"Not all the time. I really don't know, I suppose."

Luther looked up and down the street. It was deserted. No young men loitering on street corners waiting for a chance to rob someone.

"Oh, the bullet hole in our window. That's what you're thinking about. We're a liberal paper. Only one in Mississippi as far as I know. Of course we're just a weekly. That was some kids, I expect. Riding around town with a rifle. Practicing up for deer season." Chester laughed and Luther saw him watching to see if he would laugh too. Luther managed a smile. "Who knows if they were black or white? Maybe they were Mexicans? Slug got stopped by an old typewriter. The publisher was saving it as an historical curiosity. Now you go on in. Your daddy'll be back soon."

He thanked Chester for his help. Then Chester returned to the newspaper office.

Luther walked into the building and closed the door behind him. It was immediately obvious the printing company was no longer in business. As he walked through two large empty rooms, he saw marks on the cement floors where large machines had been in place. It was stifling in the rooms, and they were filled with unfamiliar smells he guessed had to do with ink and paper and machine oil. Then after searching in vain for a light switch, he made his way down a dark hallway. At the end was a door. He hesitated a moment; he felt slightly dizzy. He supposed it was the heat. For some reason he was reluctant to put his hand on the doorknob. He felt a strange desire to curl up on the floor and go to sleep as if that spot on the floor was a cool and comfortable place. But then he pushed aside this strange thought and took hold of the knob, which had a raised ornate design worked into the metal. He opened the door and stepped into an eddy of cold air. Shiny new ductwork for the air conditioning was hung from the ceiling. A set of curtainless windows looked out on the brick wall of a nearby warehouse that was perhaps twenty or thirty feet away. In the open space grew a forest of the giant weeds. At the moment the sun was in such a position that the space between the buildings was filled with a fierce glare. The weeds appeared to quiver in the heat, but he supposed that was caused by a slight breeze that had sprung up.

Now there were beautiful heart-of-pine boards beneath his feet. The furniture was spartan: a big leather-covered divan that seemed too large for the room, a lamp, a table. A stack of books, a notebook, a fountain pen, and a pistol were on the table. On the cover of the notebook, which had French words printed on it, was a picture of Hercules drawing his bow. The paper inside was lined like graph paper. He flipped through the pages. All of them were blank.

"Divan," how did he know that word? It was from his mother. In their apartment in New York there was just one small sofa, a sofa barely large enough for two people. The sofa had always seemed too small for the room. Once he had asked his mother why, and she had said she did not like those big divans. Now he realized the connection with his father's tastes. There was no TV, but there was a radio. He found a tiny kitchen and a bathroom. On the kitchen counter was a birthday cake in a box with a clear plastic top. HAPPY BIRRTHDAY 100 YEARS !!! was written in icing in the center of a circle of ten candles. His father had bought himself his own cake. He could imagine the strange exchange his father must have had with the clerk in the store. The clerk was not likely to have ever sold a cake to a very old person to give to another person who was turning one-hundred. Surely that was what the clerk must have thought were the circumstances. He wondered if those exclamation marks had been his father's idea. Then he walked through two bedrooms, each with a big divan with a lamp and table at the end of them, but in neither one was there a bed.

Everywhere there were books. Each room had floor to ceiling bookcases. He wondered if his father could still climb the small ladder in front of each bookcase to reach the upper shelves. There was what looked like a complete set of the New American Library. And a set of the French Pleiade edition. He had never known that his father could read French. The shelves were filled with translations of Russian books. There were many books on military history. It seemed to him to be a strange collection for a businessman. On one bookcase were two Russian hats. One, made of wool, had a bill and huge red star. The other was a fur hat with earflaps and a small red star. He knew his father had been in World War II. He remembered a picture of him in an officer's uniform. But he had not known his father had any connection with the Russian theatre of operations. He was tempted to try on one of the hats but decided against it.

He felt sleepy. It had been a long day. He lay down on the divan in the living room. He reached out and picked up the pistol, which was much heavier than he expected. He wondered if it was loaded. It was the kind that had a magazine in the handle, but he was unsure how to release the magazine or open the action of the gun. It might go off somehow and there would be a hole in the ceiling or wall. Then he would have to explain his ineptitude to his father. He had never fired or even handled a rifle or a pistol. The remembrance of that day he sat on the pony sprang again into his mind. He put the pistol back on the table. He closed his eyes.

The smell of food woke him. When he opened his eyes, he realized that the light was different in the room. The forest of weeds was in deep shadow. Then he saw his father standing over him. He was a tall man with a mane of white hair. In Luther's memory his father's hair was black, like his. His carriage was perfect. He did not look like someone who was going to be one-hundred years old in a few days. For a moment the thought entered Luther's mind that this was not his father at all. He wondered how long this man had been standing there, watching him sleep.

"Luther, I got us some gumbo," his father said in a deep but soft voice.

Luther did not know what to say. He was trapped between sleeping and waking. And he felt panic at sleeping so long in the unsecured apartment. Anyone could have wandered in off the street.

"Luther, Luther," his father said. "Wake up."

It did not seem to Luther that the voice he was hearing was that of an old man. It sounded young and vigorous. He wondered if he were dreaming.

Luther collected himself and sat up on the couch. Now he was certain he was awake. Then he stood up. His father was a few inches taller than he was. They stood looking at each other. Then the old man put out his arms and Luther, still half-wondering if this were a dream, allowed himself to be embraced. His father, who smelled like cigars, patted him on the back. Luther felt no conscious anger at his father for all those years of inattention, but he found it hard to feel any real affection. He wondered why he had come and at the same time felt anxious about being trapped in the apartment. He wished he had taken a room in a hotel, met his father at some neutral place, but it was too late for that now.

A big bird of some kind swooped down into the weeds. Luther

turned to follow the motion, a flash of brown and white against the green of the jungle.

"Hawk getting a rat," his father said.

Then his father looked around the apartment.

"I know this doesn't look like much," he said. "I've got a big house out at the lake with a cook and a housekeeper. They spend all their time fussing over me. That's what I pay 'em for I guess. But I like it better here. I guess most folks prefer things simpler when they get older."

Luther did not think he was going to be one of those persons. He could not understand why his father would choose to spend any time at all in the apartment. He considered the pistol. He wanted to ask if the apartment was safe but decided against it. He could imagine his father laughing at him.

They ate the gumbo, which was very good, and drank beer from his father's refrigerator. His father offered him whiskey, saying that he himself could no longer drink whiskey.

"It gives me bad dreams," he said.

Luther declined the whiskey. He would stick with beer. He would be careful not to drink too much. He did not like the idea of being drunk in this strange place. For some reason Luther could not imagine his father having bad dreams. Luther considered the bottle of Scotch and wondered if it had the same effect as whiskey on his father. His father offered him a cigar, which he declined. The old man lit one for himself, and soon a cloud of blue smoke drifted about over his head.

His father put *The Magic Flute* on the radio's disk player.

"My hearing is still perfect," his father said. "Eyesight too. I expect yours will be the same when you get as old as me."

It was just beginning to turn dark outside. The weeds had for some time been in deep shadow. Luther wondered if at night owls came to hunt the rats.

His father blew a puff of smoke toward the ceiling, and settled himself into the couch.

"I was in Russia during the war," his father said. "Attached to the American embassy. Yes, those were strange times."

He pointed to the hats on the bookshelf.

"The fur hat, the *ushanka*, was a gift from a Russian officer. The other, the one with the huge red star, is a *budenovka*. It was standard issue in nineteen seventeen. It's a copy.

"Everyone was dying around us. The Russian and German armies were at each other's throats. Stalin was killing his own people. Millions starved to death. We lived like kings."

Luther quickly calculated how old his father was then. Maybe in his late thirties. He wondered if he should ask his father something about his life in Russia. But the only question that came to Luther's mind was one concerning the depth of the snow. "How deep is the snow, Lieutenant Fisher?" It was a piece of dialogue. He was certain of that. Where had that come from? Something he had read? A movie? The sentence kept repeating itself over and over in his head. He gave up trying to remember the source. He sensed that his father, who had paused in his narrative, was waiting for a question. He was about to ask the question about the depth of the snow in Moscow when his father spoke again.

"Your stepbrothers are dead. Your stepsister is dead. Their mothers are dead."

Luther had never met his brothers and sisters. He did not want to talk about his dead relatives. He hoped his father was not going to bring up the death of his mother. Luther did not want to talk about death at all.

"But *you* are going to be one-hundred years old," Luther said.

He raised his bottle of beer and his father raised his. As they drank to his father's hundred years, Luther hoped that would be the end of talk about death.

162

"You'll live to be a hundred too," his father said. "Remember, I promised to teach you."

"I've got it in writing," Luther said.

Luther saw movement in the weeds. Something. But another big bird did not appear.

"I got the idea for these couches from Comrade Stalin," his father said. "He hardly ever slept in a bed. He'd lie down with a book on one of those big divans he kept all over the place and read himself to sleep. He was a well read man. A monster but well read."

They talked of Houston and the picture of Luther on the pony. His father claimed that he remembered that day because it was Luther's birthday. Luther began to relax.

"I remember birthdays," his father said.

Luther recalled the cards he received. There had been only one year when one had not appeared. Perhaps his father had been ill.

He was relieved when his father asked him about his work and his life in New York. Luther tried to spin out that explanation as long as possible. He gave up worrying about drinking too much. He was no longer concerned about whether his father had locked the front door of the building. They talked on and on. Then he realized that it was midnight. His father was telling him about a house trailer business he had started in Texas.

"The workers called them coaches," his father said. "They wanted to believe that they were making those fancy Airstream trailers, the ones old folks tow around the country. Then one winter they go down to Florida and die there. That won't happen to me. I'll die in one of my businesses."

Luther thought of the empty rooms once occupied by machines. It was no longer a "business," just an empty building. His father was deluding himself. But what did it matter?

Luther feared that his father was going to launch himself on a long soliloquy about death, but instead he started talking about Russia again. Luther wanted to bring up the cake. They would light the candles and cut the cake and then have one drink of the Scotch before they went to bed. He felt uncomfortable again and eagerly anticipated saying goodbye to his father and driving to the airport.

There was a knock on the door.

"It's Chester," his father said. "You go let him in."

Luther got up and went to the door, but as he started to unlock it he hesitated. There was no peephole in the door. If his father had left the front door unlocked, anyone could be standing there.

"He's got a key to the office door," his father said.

Luther opened the door and there was Chester. He had a small gift- wrapped package in his hands, the sort of package a woman whose birthday was being celebrated might expect to contain a ring or a diamond necklace.

Chester sat on the couch with them.

"Well, go get your cake," his father said. "Then I can blow out the candles and open my presents. Same thing for ninety-nine years."

Chester got up to get the cake. Luther cautioned himself to be careful from now on when he invented scenarios concerning his father. Chester returned. He brought the cake in on what looked to Luther like a piece of expensive china. Then Chester lit the candles. His father blew them out.

Luther did not know exactly what to say. He thought about living to a hundred, wondering how that would feel. But he did not want to talk about living to one hundred. So along with Chester he just said happy birthday.

"Thank you, son," his father said. "Thank you, Chester."

Luther produced his present.

"I'll open Chester's first," his father said.

He watched his father unwrap Chester's present. His father

lifted the lid off a little box and took out what looked to Luther like a lump of metal. His father held it up to the light.

"I think it was from a Wentworth rifle," Chester said.

His father explained to Luther that the rifle, a favorite of Confederate snipers during the Civil War, fired a hexagonal-shaped round.

"Where'd you find it?" his father asked.

"Vicksburg," Chester said.

"You wouldn't think it to look at him," his father said, "but Chester sneaks around the battlefield on rainy nights with a metal detector. The rangers have never come close to catching him."

Now Luther wished he had come up with a better present. He presented his father with the bottle of Scotch.

"Ah, you know this Scotch," his father said.

"Not really," Luther said. "The man in the store told me it was good."

"It's good," Chester said.

"Can you drink it?" Luther asked his father.

"I'm afraid not," his father said. "Same effect as the whiskey. I'll have to stick with German beer. You and Chester drink it."

His father opened the bottle and poured both of them a drink. Luther took up his glass.

"Smooth?" his father asked.

"Best I've ever had," Luther said.

"If I was ever going to give up drinking, I just changed my mind," Chester said.

It did taste good, but Luther knew nothing about expensive Scotch. He did not know what to say next so he again wished his father happy birthday.

"Thank you, son," his father said.

His father cut the cake. They each had a piece. They ate with silver forks off more of the fine china.

Chester told them a long story about evading park rangers. They ate more cake. Luther and Chester had another drink of Scotch. Luther felt a little drunk. He resolved not to let the Scotch turn him maudlin and foolish.

"Chester used to work for the *Herald Tribune* in Paris," his father said.

"Now I work for the newspaper with the fanciest name in Mississippi," Chester said.

"Chester is like me," his father said. "He likes things simple. He sleeps in the newspaper office on a war surplus cot. I bought that cot right after the war to take to deer camp. Comrade Lenin would approve. I never saw that cot he slept on but I heard about it. Stalin and Lenin. There was something about beds they just didn't like."

Luther wondered what Chester's life had been like when he lived in Paris. Perhaps Chester and his father sat around drinking beer and smoking expensive cigars and discussing the French books in his father's collection. What chain of events had brought Chester to Mississippi to live in a newspaper office?

Chester pressed another glass of Scotch on Luther and he accepted. His father and Chester lit up cigars. When his father offered Luther one he took it. He puffed on it, careful not to draw the smoke into his lungs.

As his father began to tell another story about Russia during the war, Luther realized that he had taken one drink too many. He was having trouble following his father's story. It was something about a frozen lake. But he decided he did not care. For the moment he would just drift among the stories of his father's past. In the morning he would ask him particular questions about his mother. How had they met? Why had the marriage failed? Why, when Luther was a child, did his father not invite him down to Mississippi or Texas or wherever he was living? He could have learned to ride real horses in Texas.

"Listen to Chester, Luther," his father was saying. "Listen."

Luther focused on the pair, both of them sitting at one end of the sofa and he at the other.

"I believe a heavy morning dew has fallen on this boy," his father said.

"No more Scotch," Chester said.

"Listen," his father said.

Then Chester began to tell a story told to him when he was in Finland. For some reason Luther could not imagine Chester in Finland or even outside of Mississippi. *But he lived in Paris,* Luther told himself, *probably for years. You've never lived in Paris. So listen.* Luther only could understand bits and pieces of it. He did not understand what Chester was doing in Finland. The story had been told to him by a young Finnish psychiatrist.

"It was cold there," Chester said. "So cold the ocean froze. The ice was blue."

Then Luther made the mistake of trying to imagine the color of the ice, the depth of it and so lost contact with the story.

"Hesperia, the Hospital of the Night, was where that young doctor was working," Chester said.

Luther concentrated hard, trying to step into the flow of the story again.

Chester went on to explain how a patient speaking some unknown language had been brought in out of the snow naked and in restraints. The staff was mystified. Then one day he started to speak Russian to the young doctor. It turned out he had been a KGB operative in Afghanistan.

"It was some weird dialect from one of those provinces in the Hindu Kush he was speaking," Chester said. "They'd trained him so well that when he went crazy he still kept his cover."

"What happened to the KGB man?" his father asked.

"The young doctor didn't know," Chester said. "He got

transferred to Aurora, the Hospital of the Morning. I guess he got caught up in his work. Forgot to ask."

His father began to laugh.

"The Hospital of the Morning," he said. "You're making this up."

"No, I swear it's true," Chester said.

"This Finn had good English?"

"Perfect. Better than yours."

"And he *never* found out what happened to the Russian."

"He said he never did. Said he was distracted by difficult patients at the Hospital of the Morning."

"What do you think, Luther?"

"He's too drunk to know what he thinks," Chester said.

Luther agreed with Chester.

"I believe the part about it being cold in Finland in the winter," he said.

His father and Chester laughed. Chester poured himself another drink. Luther wondered if they planned on staying up all night. His plane left in mid-afternoon. He was beginning to worry about making it. He wanted to wake up early enough to talk seriously with his father. Maybe they would talk about his mother. He announced that he was going to sleep.

"There're blankets in the closet if you get cold," his father said.

Luther walked unsteadily toward the bedrooms. He did not like the idea of waking up in the morning to a close-up view of the giant weeds through the curtainless windows.

Once he reached the bedroom, he kicked off his shoes, pulled off his socks, and lay down on the couch. The light from the rising moon illuminated the weeds, which to him seemed as tall as redwoods. He turned his head away from them.

Sleep did not come as easily as he expected. Through the open door he heard the voices of his father and Luther. He smelled their cigars. Or perhaps, he thought, it was the smell of the smoke on his clothes. He felt a desire to brush his teeth, to get the tobacco taste out of his mouth. But he was too tired to get up. He found himself wondering if the two men who slept alone in offices were ever sad and lonely. He knew he would be. Then he finally slept.

He woke. His father was standing over him, the moonlight caught up in his white hair. His father said something that Luther could not understand as he spread a blanket over him. Then his father was gone and Luther gratefully slipped back into a dreamless sleep.

***

Luther was awakened by an enormous sound. The room was full of light. He turned and faced the window. The sunlight-bathed forest of weeds sprang into view. His concern for what the sound meant and his sudden anxiety about missing his flight merged and spun about in his mind. It was with considerable difficulty that he focused on the sound, which did not come again. He heard someone's feet on the floor.

"Goddamn! Goddamn!"

It was his father's voice.

He now realized that the sound had been a gunshot. The only explanation could be that his father had shot an intruder. Chester had gone home drunk and had forgotten to lock the door of the office. His father had done the same with the apartment door. He imagined someone lying in a pool of blood on the floor before the big divan in the living room. He looked for his shoes but could locate only one. He gave up on the missing shoe and went barefoot toward the living room. The pine boards felt cool and slick beneath his feet.

When he reached the living room, he saw nothing, not the

body he expected. A blanket was on the floor. The pistol was not on the table. The door to the apartment was closed. As he took at step toward the door, he heard footsteps in the bedroom. So someone had come in from the forest of weeds through one of the windows.

He cautiously looked around the corner of the bedroom door. His father had his back to him. He had no pants on. Luther was struck by the thinness of his father's legs and how white they were. His father turned to look at him. His hands were empty.

"Look at this," he said. "Look at this."

Then Luther saw someone on the divan. His father had shot an intruder while he slept on the divan? Then as he came closer he saw it was Chester. He looked like he was asleep.

"Put the barrel in his mouth," his father said. "I'm sure the back of his head is gone."

His father reached down and pulled a blanket over Chester's face.

Then his father explained to Luther how Chester had asked him if he could spend the night.

"Why didn't he just go on back to the newspaper office and do it there?" his father said. "Why here?"

Chester had obviously awakened early and had taken the pistol from the table while his father slept. Luther imagined him lying there on the couch all night contemplating suicide. When the weeds finally filled with light, he had made up his mind. His father showed him the note Chester had written on the second page of the notebook.

Tell that boy the way to live to be one-hundred is not to shoot yourself.

"Now what in the hell does that mean?" his father asked. "What kind of suicide note is that? Why'd he do it on my birthday?"

They retreated to the living room to await the arrival of the police. As they drank coffee, they discussed Chester's possible motives. It turned out that his father did not know much about Chester. He had come to the apartment a few times for a drink. The purchase of the cake had been a complete surprise. It was clear to Luther that they were not close friends.

The police, who knew his father, asked a few questions and took away the body. By that time it was a little after midday.

Luther had to go to the airport. His father told Luther that he was going back to his house on the lake. He would sell the printing office. He would have his books moved, maybe to the house.

"I'm having another birthday party at the lake, on Wednesday," he said. "Maybe you could fly down for that. I'll buy you a ticket. You could stay through the weekend. We could talk."

Luther said he would think about it, let his father know. He was not sure what he was going to do. The Hospital of the Morning. Blue ice. What was Chester's purpose in telling them that story? Or maybe there was no purpose. He was just drunk. And Chester's note. What about that? Above all he would ponder carefully the proposed visit to his father as he flew back to New York in the brilliant air, high above the fields and towns and cities.

Guatemala City

Cassie lay in bed beside her husband Rembert. She placed her palm on his back between his shoulder blades. His body beneath her hand was lean and solid, the body of an athlete. She considered embracing him, of pressing herself close to him, but if she did that he might wake and they would make love. Right now she simply wanted to think about having him in bed with her. Making love would spoil that.

She liked lying beside him in the morning, particularly because it had not yet been a year since he had returned from Vietnam. She had never thought he would not return, because her childhood friend Peter, who was also Rembert's friend, had assured her nothing would happen to Rembert, that people like Rembert always survived. She had embraced what Peter told her just as firmly as a religious enthusiast might cling to a promise of eternal life from her god.

Rembert had returned home to Mississippi with a medal for bravery under fire but no Purple Heart because he had not received so much as a scratch during his tour. Peter had also predicated that Rembert would be like Achilles, invulnerable to the weapons of his enemies. And as far as she could tell there were no psychic wounds. Rembert slept soundly, better than she, troubled by no bad dreams.

They had come to Guatemala to buy Mayan art. She knew it was illegal, but it was not a *serious* crime. The farmers and hunters who discovered the art needed the money, and Rembert paid everyone well.

"I'm not stealing, I'm buying," Rembert liked to say. "There's a difference."

It made her uncomfortable. It had been different when he went off alone. After he returned from that first trip, they suddenly had money and to continue having that sort of money it was logical he would have to continue "buying." Being in the place where the art originated gave her a different sort of view, one that made her more than vaguely anxious. But she liked it that he took her along, that he wanted her close to him. This trip was like a honeymoon. They had taken a suite in the best hotel in town.

Rembert presented the appearance that he had come to Guatemala to hunt jaguars and actually did go on several hunts. The skin of the best cat he had shot would be shipped to New Orleans along with a crate of vases depicting Mayan ball games. There was absolutely no danger, he had told her. His cousin, a doctor in New Orleans, had been treating a government official who had arranged the jaguar hunts, the same official who made it possible for Rembert to buy the vases.

He had wanted to go back to Vietnam or Cambodia to buy art, but right now those places were too hot. That was why Rembert had volunteered for the army, for dangerous recon work, so he could locate new sources, temples hidden deep in the rain forests of the highlands. Rembert's hero was André Malraux, who along with his wife had been so brazen as to attempt to dismantle a temple in Cambodia. The Malrauxs had failed and had narrowly escaped a prison sentence. Rembert had not found a single temple during his tour of duty. He still wanted to go there later, after the war. Rembert claimed he did not care which side won, but he hoped it was the South Vietnamese because they would be easier to deal with than the Communists. He told her that he intended to use much of the money he made to finance archeological expeditions, in imitation of his hero Malraux, but so far that had not happened. Instead they had bought a house, cars, and an airplane.

She was not troubled by the danger involved, the chance there were people who would take by force the vases for which Rembert had been willing to pay a fair market price. He carried a pistol, a dark blue German thing, in a shoulder holster. It was war booty. His father had taken it from a dead German officer somewhere in Romania during World War II. Rembert slept with it under his pillow.

Instead of Peter's reassuring her that nothing would happen to Rembert, she had decided for herself this time. But she was worried about earthquakes and volcanic eruptions. From the balcony outside their room, she could see the *Volcan de Agua*, whose eruption had destroyed the old colonial capital at the end of the eighteenth century. The sunset the day before had been spectacular. Pacaya, a volcano to the left of Agua, had been in constant eruption for several years, throwing up clouds of ash which created the lovely sunsets. She still had not seen the others, Fuego and Acatenango, which flanked Agua on the right.

Rembert groaned his sleep. She removed her hand from his back. She did not want him to wake. But instead of lying there and watching him sleep, she drifted off herself. She slept and did not dream.

***

They had breakfast on the balcony. It was pleasant in the sunlight, not yet grown hot. The outline of Agua was made indistinct by the ash-filled air. She knew that if the air were clear, Agua's immense bulk would have made the hotel feel small and vulnerable.

"Don't worry," Rembert said. "Nothing's going to happen while we're here."

He was departing for his final hunt later in the day. He would be gone three days.

"I never worry about floods at home," she said. "I wonder why volcanoes unsettle me."

Once, when she was a child, the water had come up out of the slough. Her father used a front-end loader to build a dike around the house but the hastily built dike failed. They went out to high ground in a skiff. It was a bright sunny day, the blue April sky incongruous with the flat expanse of muddy water. The water was not still, not like a pond, but flowed off to the southwest with a slow but steady current. Toward a break in the levee, her father observed. There was an enormous power in it, a power that frightened her parents, even her father. She was not frightened at all and comforted her mother, who was crying over her ruined furniture.

"Go shopping today," Rembert said. "Buy yourself something nice."

It seemed incredible to her that her husband had bought on the black market the vases that would be converted into large sums of money so they could have a beautiful life in New Orleans and that they were sitting having breakfast on this balcony with the view of the volcano that might at any moment spew forth lava and ash, burying them like the citizens of Pompeii.

"Would we be worth anything if we were buried by the volcano?" she asked. "Like at Pompeii. Those plaster casts of the dead."

"If enough time passed," he said. "We wouldn't be worth much."

They would not keep even one of those beautiful vases for their private collection. That was a rule he had made, to keep nothing for themselves.

"Nothing's going to happen," he said. "There'll be no Pompeii here. I want to hunt one more time. Mr. Alvarado has seen the tracks of a big cat on his hacienda."

"Mr. Alvarado lost an eye to a jaguar," she said. "Remember, I want you back safe."

"That won't happen to me. You know it won't."

She had long ago abandoned the religion of her parents, Episcopalians, whose god always seemed to her gray and dull, like a stretch of bottom land in winter. Rembert's invulnerability was their religion.

"I know," she said, thinking as she spoke that her reply was a piece of their private liturgy, affirming their belief in the safety of both of them.

They finished breakfast and he went downstairs to meet the car sent by Mr. Alvarado. At the airport Mr. Alvarado's private plane was waiting.

***

She went off to go shopping, not at all sure what she would buy. It was possible to take almost anything back on the boat with them. She looked at carved colonial chests in a shop. But she could not make up her mind. She had lunch and then sat and drank coffee in a café and smoked cigarettes.

Now she wished she had gone hunting with Rembert. He had offered to take her. She imagined the green rain forest and how a jaguar with golden eyes would suddenly materialize out of that green. She had not asked Rembert if they used dogs like they did for deer in Mississippi. She was a good shot. Rembert had taught her to shoot. Every deer she had taken she had killed cleanly with one shot.

From time to time she considered how her parents might react if they found out what Rembert was doing. But they had no idea where the money was coming from. They already disapproved of

176

Rembert's being what he called a "military consultant" to foreign governments.

"What if he had gone to work for the CIA?" she told her father. "You would have thought that was all right."

"He'd be working for America," her father said. "He's working for himself. What's he doing?"

"I don't know," she lied.

It made her uncomfortable lying to her father.

"I wish you'd make him tell you," he said. "Then *you* decide if it's something your children will be proud of."

She did not tell her father that she and Rembert did not plan to have children. Her mother gave her little trouble. She liked the fact they were able to buy a house in the Garden District in New Orleans. She had been brought up to not concern herself with how men made money.

Rembert's father (his mother was dead), who had expected Rembert to go back to Harvard and finish his degree and return to help him sell cotton, rice, and soybeans on the world market, threatened to remove his only son from his will when one night after dinner Rembert used the phrase "military consultant" to describe his work.

"A goddamn mercenary," Mr. Williams had said. "You're going to end up in some foreign jail. Don't come whining to me to help you get out."

She wished she were not in the room with them and got up to leave.

"Are you going to let him do that?" Mr. Williams asked her.

"If he wants to do it, he should do it," she said.

Mr. Williams walked out of the room in disgust.

She returned to her shopping. She wandered into a shop that sold birds. There she bought a parrot. It was a bird that the owner of the shop said he himself had caught in the forest on the slopes of the volcano. But although the parrot refused to make a single sound while she was there, he assured her the bird was a good talker, a singer of songs. As she arranged to have the bird delivered to the hotel, she imagined Rembert teasing her for buying a parrot that refused to speak.

Instead of taking a cab, she decided to walk back to the hotel. As she rounded a corner, she saw a couple disappearing into a hotel. She saw the woman clearly, but she caught only a brief glimpse of the man. Although she was several hundred yards away, she was certain the man was Rembert. Suddenly it seemed to her that there was not enough oxygen in the air. It was like she had been transported to the top of the volcano, where the air was thin and cold.

As she walked toward the hotel entrance where a doorman was stationed, she took slow deep breaths to calm herself. She thought of her mother and father quarreling over his going turkey hunting. She imagined she must have been twelve or thirteen at the time. They thought she was asleep but she had been awakened by their angry voices and had come out of her room to sit at the top of the stairs.

"Barbara Masone saw you," her mother said.

"She saw somebody else," her father said. "I was hunting. I've got the mosquito bites to prove it."

"That woman," her mother said. "You were with that woman."

"Libby, it was somebody else she saw. You know Barbara likes to take a drink. That's what she was doing at the Holiday Inn. Everybody knows she's at that bar every afternoon. Now why would any married man in this town take a woman there?"

Her mother had muttered something Cassie could not make out. Then she heard her mother sobbing and her father talking gently to her.

Later she discovered her mother's suspicions were true. But that was the last time she ever heard her mother confront her father. Her mother drank too much and sometimes, late in the afternoon after a day of drinking from bottles she had stashed all over the house, she complained of her husband's lack of attention, but she never said a word to Cassie about other women.

"I don't like Charles being gone so much," she would say. "But he has to make a living."

Yet everyone in town knew her father was always involved with some woman and that finally her mother chose to ignore them, to pretend they did not exist at all.

Cassie walked past the doorman in his magnificent uniform and into the lobby, a splendid one full of glass and marble. People were sitting on plush sofas and in the bar a solitary barman was drying glasses with a towel. She went up to the desk and asked if anyone spoke English. The young desk clerk carefully told her in his uncertain English that he would call the manager, who spoke excellent English. He picked up a telephone and spoke a few words into it. She waited at the desk while he stood there and smiled at her.

She was relieved when a man and his wife appeared at the desk and he devoted his attention to them. She began to realize how foolish she was being. She had no idea what she was going to say to the manager. She could not ask him if he had seen someone who looked like her husband stroll across the lobby with another woman. How could she say that she thought, only *thought* she had seen her husband, who was supposed to be jaguar hunting a hundred miles away. And since they were not in the lobby and not in the bar, she supposed they were in a room somewhere right now, in bed, or having a drink together and preparing to be in bed. That is if it were Rembert she had seen and not some other man with blond hair. But how could she say any of this with her little Spanish when it would have been difficult enough to say to the manager of the Peabody Hotel in Memphis. She considered walking out of the hotel.

Now she felt as if there were too much oxygen in the air. The blood surged through her body. She would not be like her mother. She would confront Rembert. For the first time it became clear to her how a woman might shoot her unfaithful husband or his lover. But she could not understand how her mother had managed to shut her jealously away in some secret place in her heart.

A door behind the desk opened and the manager appeared.

"May I assist you, Señora?" the manager asked.

He was old enough to have been her father. She paused for a moment to compose herself. The two men stood there staring at her.

"Are there Americans staying at this hotel?" she asked.

"Yes, Señora," he said.

The younger clerk was looking at her in what she thought was a disapproving way. There was a hint of a smile on his lips.

"I mean . . .you see," she began. "My friend Mr. Clark often comes here on business."

"He stays at this hotel?" the man asked.

"No, not here. He stays at others."

"Then why are you looking for him here?"

Now she was certain the young clerk was mocking her.

"I thought I saw him on the street," she said. "He is a tall man with blond hair. A young man."

The young clerk said something to the manager in Spanish.

"Did he come in here with a woman?" the manager asked.

"Yes," she said.

"That was Herr Herder," he said. "He and his wife come here often."

She apologized and knew that she was blushing and that both the manager and the young clerk had guessed why she was asking questions. She thanked them both and went out of the hotel. But by the time she had crossed the street and was on her way back to her hotel she began to doubt that the manager was telling her the truth. So she walked back along the street. Exhausted she took a seat in a café several blocks from the hotel. It was hot now; her whole body felt heavy.

There she sat under an umbrella all afternoon drinking coffee and watching people go through the hotel's revolving doors. By late afternoon she had drunk too much coffee and doubted whether she would be able to sleep that night. She had not seen Herr Herder and his wife come out of the hotel. She imagined they had gone up to their room and had taken a siesta. She wished they would come out on one of the balconies, where flowers grew in window boxes. The balconies on the front of the hotel were now in the shade and they might stand there and smoke cigarettes and look at the volcano. But she was not sure she could tell if it were Rembert from such a distance. She would have to walk down the street until she was directly in front of the hotel.

Then she saw the woman, a tall woman with dark hair, slim enough to be a model, emerge from the revolving doors. She paused for a moment as she adjusted her hat. Cassie was more than a hundred yards away, not close enough to make out any details of her face. At the same time a car pulled up in front of the hotel. A driver sprang out and opened the door. A moment later the man followed. Although she only caught a glimpse of him, she was sure it was Rembert who crossed the space between the revolving door and the open door of the car and disappeared into it. Unfortunately the car drove off in the opposite direction. As soon as it was gone she again began to doubt what she had seen. Any tall blond man could easily be transformed into Rembert by her imagination.

I'm seeing what I want to see, she thought. *But why would I want to see that?*

She could imagine her mother's reaction if she had come upon her father strolling into the Peabody Hotel with a woman on his arm. She was sure that her father still saw women in Memphis or New Orleans. Her mother would have pretended not to have seen him at all.

"I won't be like her," she said. "I won't."

The couple at the table next to her were staring at her, their coffee cups half raised, arrested by the sight of an American woman talking to herself.

***

At the hotel she found the parrot waiting for her in a cage at the front desk. It was amusing the staff by singing pieces of songs. From time to time it produced the siren. The desk clerk told her that they were love songs, ones which everyone in the city knew by heart. The parrot started another song and the clerk and the bellhops laughed.

"Do not be alarmed, Señora Williams," the clerk said. "They are not profane songs."

A bellhop carried the cage up to the room for her. She made herself a drink and took at long bath while the parrot sang love songs from his cage on the balcony. She tried not to think about Rembert. But that was impossible and again she began to question what she had seen. Right now Rembert was probably far away on the hacienda and not at the hotel, lying in bed with the dark-haired woman.

After her bath she had another drink and then lay in bed and read. Once it grew dark she brought the parrot inside and covered his cage. She ordered dinner sent up. She ate a few bites of the excellent meal but had no appetite. She called and had the dinner taken away. She tried to read but found she could not concentrate. She drank half of the bottle of wine. Rembert would not call. He was at a hunting cabin where there was no phone. She put the book away and sat on the end of the bed and drank the rest of the wine. She went to bed pleasantly drunk, hoping she would sleep soundly and not wake with a hangover.

***

She did sleep soundly and woke with a clear head at first light. She carried the parrot's cage out onto the balcony. The sky was hazy. Over toward the volcanoes the haze was more dense, probably thickened by a new cloud of ash thrown up by Pacaya. She could not see Agua. The sound of a few cars drifted up to her from the street. When she removed the cover from the bird's cage, the parrot sat there calmly and made no sound. Then it imitated a car's horn and she laughed. She imagined Rembert awakening in the company of hunters. Now she felt foolish about her suspicions.

She had breakfast and went out to shop. She still wanted to find a carved trunk. And she managed to lose herself in the excitement of her search until after lunch when she found herself sitting in the same café close to the hotel. Now the same fierce jealously filled her as when she had first seen a tall blond man walk into the hotel with a woman.

All afternoon she sat there but was rewarded with no sighting. And by late afternoon, when she returned to the hotel with the matter of the trunk still not settled and feeling shaky from too much coffee, she was furious with herself. She made herself a martini and took another long bath while the parrot, who still did not have a name, sang love songs from the balcony. The bird was delighted at her return, greeting her with soft whistles. It had sat on her arm while she fed it a nut.

After her bath she had dinner in the room and drank another bottle of wine. She brought the bird's cage into the room and covered it. As she lay in bed and waited for sleep to come, she tried to imagine Rembert going to sleep in the hunting cabin. If thoughts of her were not in his mind then perhaps he was thinking of a fine jaguar he had just shot as he too drifted off to sleep.

***

In the morning she found the trunk she was looking for. The shop owner claimed it had once held the silver and linens of a viceroy's wife. The elaborate carving on the lid made her certain that if it had not belonged to a viceroy's wife at least its owner had been someone important.

Rembert would return that evening and she eagerly anticipated his coming. She wondered if she would be able to smell the rain forest on him, a scent of dead leaves not unlike that of the river bottoms at home in Mississippi, and would know for sure he had spent the last three days at the hacienda.

She wandered about the city. She considered buying an emerald necklace in a shop, but she ended up buying nothing. By mid-afternoon she found herself close to the café where for two days she had sat and watched the hotel. She decided to have a coffee and pretend this was the first time she had visited it. It would be a sort of cure against jealously, against imagining things that might not be true. Rembert was not her father.

The waiters greeted her when she stepped off the street. She did not choose a table with a view of the hotel but deliberately sat with her back to the street. She sat there and thought about where she might place the trunk in the new house. After she finished her coffee, she left, enormously pleased that she had put her jealously behind her. She decided to walk past the hotel, a route she did not have to take, because the way to her hotel lay in the other direction.

That will be the final cure for this, she thought.

She was on the other side of the street when she approached the hotel. When she drew opposite the door, she stopped and turned to face it. The doorman stood at his post. He nodded at her and she at him. She looked up at the rooms with their flower-covered balconies, hoping to see Herr Herder and his elegant wife.

Then the revolving doors went round and for a moment she wondered if Herr Herder was going to appear. She imagined herself walking over to get a close look at him. Perhaps his wife would come through the doors and she could meet her too. She would introduce herself and they would all stroll down to the café and have a drink. Instead it was the young desk clerk. The doorman turned to face him, but the clerk ignored him and smiled at her, that salacious, knowing smile. She felt herself blushing. She turned and walked off down the street in the direction of her hotel. She was certain she heard the men laughing.

***

Rembert had shot a fine jaguar, even better than the one already prepared for shipment home. He told her about the hunt as they lay in bed together. He had a scratch on his upper arm from a thorn. After he took a long bath she cleaned the wound for him and painted it with iodine. He had received it that morning on his final hunt. He had come home dirty and unshaven, smelling, to her great joy, of dead leaves.

After love they lay in bed together and Rembert drifted off to sleep. He slept soundly, the sleep of a man who had hunted long and hard or, she thought, it was the sleep of a man who had spent three days in bed with a woman.

She put her nose into his hair to see if she could smell some hint of a woman's perfume or the scent of her sex. Rembert's hair was cut short in opposition to the style of the day. She recalled pictures he sent her of himself when he was in Vietnam, sometimes perched on a wall of sandbags with a rifle in his hands or standing with a group of soldiers, all their faces painted with camouflage. She sniffed the length of his body. At his groin there was the scent of sex, her scent too. She could smell nothing not familiar. If there had been marks from a woman's nails or teeth on him, she would have known that he had been in the city the whole time and not jaguar hunting at all. And it seemed to her that he had made love to her with the sort of enthusiasm of a man who had been away from his wife for several days.

He woke.

"What are you doing?" he asked. "I need to sleep. We have to get up early tomorrow."

They were scheduled to take the train to Puerto Barrios the next day and then a boat to New Orleans.

"Looking at you," she said.

He kissed her. She ran her fingers over the scratch. He had refused to put a bandage on it. He said it needed air.

"I hope it won't get infected," she said.

"I don't infect," he said. "Remember when I rode my bicycle into that barbed wire fence. I was cut up good. Nothing got infected. They told me people get scratched from that sort of thorn all the time. It's nothing."

"I don't want anything to happen to you. Ever."

"Nothing will. Remember Peter the Prophet's prediction. My father is still complaining I didn't get a Purple Heart."

"Not seriously."

"No, but he has two."

I know it was him, she thought. *Now why can't I just say that to him? And would I leave him if he admitted it was true?*

For the first time she saw her mother's predicament clearly, one for which she had never had much sympathy.

The parrot began to sing a love song. Rembert had immediately named the bird Rudyard. Rembert was a great lover of Kipling.

186

"How can you be sure they're love songs?" Rembert asked.

"I don't know," she said. "I suppose you have to trust people."

"That bird is probably singing obscene ballads it learned in brothels."

She marveled at how Rembert, who spoke little Spanish, could make a statement like this. He once pointed out that it was going to be impossible to learn all the necessary languages. And besides he had no talent for languages. Survival was his talent. He planned on getting by with a little Spanish and even less French.

"Perhaps," she said. "I don't think the desk clerk would lie to me."

"Maybe he was just being polite," he said.

"They sound too tender to be those sorts of songs."

Rembert got out of bed and put the cover over the parrot's cage. He turned off the lights and walked back across the room to the bed in the dark. Then they went to sleep. As she lay with her arms around Rembert, he sound asleep, she realized she was sure it had been her husband she had seen with the woman. She rolled away from him and lay on her back, her arms at her side and her legs together. The man she had seen had walked exactly the same way Rembert did when he walked across the room in the dark. It was a hunter's walk, a soldier's walk, his feet coming down with certainty but always ready to dance away from a snake or a booby trap in his path. And she knew she was going to say nothing to him about it. Instead, she was going to try harder to make herself exciting to him. She would be a companion in his smuggling of art. It would be as if she were a man. He would not be able to find another woman like her. And if he persisted in his pursuit of other women she would not be patient like her mother. She would leave him.

I won't be like Mother, she thought. *I won't.*

And she lay there, her whole body rigid, willing her muscles to relax one by one so she could sleep.

Scott Ely was raised in Jackson, Mississippi. He served in Vietnam as an infantryman. He received his MFA from the University of Arkansas. For the past twenty-three years, he has been teaching writing in South Carolina at Winthrop University. He has published five novels and three collections of short stories and is the recipient of a National Endowment for the Arts Fellowship and a Rockefeller Fellowship to Bellagio, Italy.